MW01639651

Just Beyond

My Heart

Lies My Soul

By

Tonya Jordan

Infinity

Publishing

ISBN 0-7414-2221-2

Published by:

INFINITY
PUBLISHING.COM

1094 New DeHaven Street, Suite 100
West Conshohocken, PA 19428-2713
Info@buybooksontheweb.com
www.buybooksontheweb.com
Toll-free (877) BUY BOOK
Local Phone (610) 941-9999
Fax (610) 941-9959

Printed in the United States of America

Printed on Recycled Paper

Published September 2004

This book is dedicated to my two daughters Whittney Tillman and Chelsie Halsel. Two of the kindest people I know. Thank you for supporting me as I go after dream, after dream, after dream. I know that some ideas make no sense, however you are always ready to offer words of encouragement. You two are an extension of me and it makes me proud that I'm apart of you.

May God continue to bless you both on your own individual dreams. Keep God first. Ask for His blessings and you will not go wrong.

Who loves you…?

Mommy

Acknowledgements

Thank you my Heavenly Father for all your guidance in my life and on this project. Thank you for the vision of this book. Thank you for allowing me such an honor and opportunity. What a blessing! Father, I ask your blessings upon this book and that you have favor upon my efforts to aid in awareness of Domestic Violence.

Thank you my dear friend and sister here on earth, Marian Hawkins, for your continued support and encouragement, and prayers.

Thank you to Anna Glenn for all your help, for taking on this project. It's hard to find someone who is interested in someone else's dream. This project would not be the same without your spirit. Thank you!

Thank you to all my readers who have helped me with the process from beginning to end. Thank you for all your suggestions, comments and concerns. Your opinions were very important to me.

Thank you to my dear friend/co-worker, Rachelle Adams "Shelly", for spiritual Guidance. Also for your continued support and encouragement, "Believe."

Thank you to my family for your words of encouragement and allowing me to share my most inner feelings on family issues and events.

Thank you to my sister, my advocate at the Center for Women and Families. Thanks for pushing me to explore my writing, and challenging myself.

Thank you to the staff at the Center for Women and Families for saving my life and allowing my children and I a safe place to start anew.

Special thanks to my father James Holt and my grandfather, Jimmie Campbell for being great role models to my girls and myself.

Thank you to all my sisters and brothers that were living at the center during my stay in the summer of 2003. Thanks for welcoming me.

Thank you to my co-workers for all your support and words of encouragement.

Most of all thank you my two beautiful daughters for sharing me with the rest of the world and allowing the world to see us.

Thanks to Will, for helping me see myself.

Thank you, Mrs. Shirley, for always being there.

Thank you to my pastor, Michael Priester and his wife, Jesse Priester for encouraging me to be the best I can be and always opening your home and your heart.

Thanks Dr. Drae'. Ya know who ya are!

God bless you all!

In Loving Memory

To my mother, Susie Holt, I love you momma. I think about you and pray for you often.

To my grandmother, Ruth Campbell, I love you granny. I miss you dearly.

To my uncle, Jimmie Campbell, Jr. "Big Jim", I love you.

To James Campbell "Jamie", I love you.

To Debra Wright, a dear friend of mine. I miss you Debbie.

To all the women who lost their lives to domestic violence.

A Letter of Dedication to My Sisters

I would personally like to apologize to all of you for the pain that you have endured. I would like to give you a hug and tell you that I love you.

I will put you in my thoughts tonight, and I welcome your thoughts.

It is very important that we stick together and support one another.

Practice random acts of kindness; offer words of encouragement to another sister.

I would like to stress to you that you can do anything that you allow yourself to do and that you can grow and heal if you allow yourself to.

Now is the time to forgive yourself and anyone else that may have caused you pain.

Now is the time for you to take steps to begin healing. Do not be afraid to ask for help. Be patient with yourself and others, healing will not come overnight.

To me you are very special and you deserve the best.

Sometimes you have to give yourself what you wish you could get from others:

Love,

Kindness,

Forgiveness,

A smile,

A compliment.

Ya see right now at this moment in your life, it is your time and it's all about you. Take time for you, be there for you, and believe in you and most of all:

BE YOU!!!

Always thinking about you,

Rhonda (A survivor of domestic violence)

Contents

DOWN ON THIRTY FOURTH STREET

While Roderick and I dated, he spent many days and nights down on Thirty-Fourth Street. Sometimes it was by choice. Sometimes it was because I put him out. Sometimes it was her luring him in. It was like a magic spell that he himself was under. He had told me of a girl that he had met say, eleven years ago. And when I met him, he wasn't into her then. As a matter of fact, she had been on vacation for an entire week. He didn't call her or even spend time with her. He told me he was bored with the relationship.

To be honest, he told me that the Thanksgiving Day that he and I met, she had prepared a huge meal for him and her daughters. And he was a no show because he chose to spend the day with me to get to know me. He stood her up. This obviously had his mom shocked because he didn't go. His mom assumed that they had been arguing.

This girl was named Rashida. They had met each other while Roderick was going through a divorce. Roderick was sleeping on the couch and his wife; Yasmine was in the other room. Roderick told me that he was working at a local grocery store preparing taxes. Another lady friend of his told him of a girlfriend of hers that he should meet. Sooo, they did. Rashida prepared supper for Roderick and they started to get to know each other. From that point on, they started seeing each other on a regular basis. They began a bond of friendship and intimacy. Over the years, they would live together, make up and break up. But they had a bond. Rashida would always allow Roderick a place to stay if he needed to. They were in fact soul mates and would be there for each other, until he met me.

I was the girl that caused the threat to their relationship. They both would venture off and date others over the years but somehow would always end back up with each other. Rashida had been a part of all of Roderick's girlfriend's lives. And Rashida always knew that Roderick would be back because he had problems with commitments and Rashida knew that. She always knew that he'd be around. At times, he would disappear for months and even years. But was always glad to see him and be with him. The reason that I know is because Rashida and I have actually talked on the phone on several occasions. Hmmm, Roderick's two ladies talking on the phone, about him no doubt.

One Saturday morning, my daughters, Roderick, and I headed over to his mom's house. We even took the dog. The girls and I were to spend the morning getting to know his mother better and just enjoying a

Saturday afternoon with his family. Roderick and I had dated, I'd say for about six months now.

Things were pretty good other than an occasional argument here and there. Every now and then, he'd stay out all night, and come in apologizing all over himself. So, right now things were a bit shaky. But, what new relationship is not- or, any relationship for that matter. No one knows what the future holds.

So, while we were visiting his mom, Roderick would be leaving to go and help an old friend do some odds and ends work on some property his friend Ray was renting out. Roderick would make some money. We'd have money for groceries, and entertainment.

Roderick was living with me the majority of the time and would on occasion go back to stay in his room in his mothers basement. Especially, when we would fall out with each other or if we were getting on each other's nerves.

So the girls and I started helping mom around the kitchen and assisting her with Sunday's dinner. Also fixing our lunch for the day. We began looking at old photos of the family and just really having a relaxing time. Roderick's mother and I would talk about his past and the things that he had been through in his life. It was sorta of a Roderick course. I enjoyed seeing and hearing things about him when he was a child.

Roderick had just recently stayed out overnight. I was expressing to his mother how it had hurt me and that I wouldn't allow such things. She and I would exchange ideas on how to approach the situation. While the girls were in the other room watching videos on the TV, she and I really began to talk and share with each other. She went on to explain that he had not been the same man after the break up with his ex-wife, Yasmine. The fact they really had a nice life together. When he was going through his court issues, due to someone stealing his identity, and going through it with the Federal Government and the impact it had on his life as of late.

So we were just having a great time and enjoying the day. Knock. Knock, "Come in," mom said.

The door opened, but we didn't know who it was.

We heard a soft voice saying, "It's me, Rashida."

And we both, mom and I, looked kinda shocked. I had only heard about her briefly, but never seen or met her. So she came in, spoke, and asked mom to go off in private. So they went into another room and talked just for about two or three minutes. Then she came out and left. The look on mom's face was in awe.

She said, “That was Rashida. And she came to bring Roderick's wallet. He evidently left it over a few days ago.”

I was shocked too. But I knew that he and I would have to discuss this. So, mom and I continued to talk.

About an hour later, Roderick comes in and says, “Hey Babe. What’s up?”

And I say, "You and Rashida."

“Whatcha talking about?”

“Well, you had a visitor while you were gone. She came over to bring your wallet. I'm sure hoping to see you as well.”

So mom excused herself. The girls by then had gone outside. So, it left us to talk.

Roderick said, “I don't want to be with her.”

I said, “Oh, but you'd go and stay all night and sleep with her?”

He said, “No, I slept on the floor. We just sat up all night and talked.”

I was very upset. I told him that he needed to make a choice, me or her.

He said that she wasn't the one he wanted to be with and she was not the type to be in a relationship or to marry. He was through with her.

So, I forgave him and we continued to have a great day, as well as the rest of the weekend. But deep inside, I was really feeling that he was full of bull. I knew that this was just the beginning of Rashida being in our lives and I may as well get ready. But, I wouldn't dare share that with him.

It began to be a routine that every time Roderick and I would fall out, that he would go running to Rashida. He would stay out all night and come in as if he was out with the guys. I knew when he had seen or talked to her, because he would call me, “Rashida” by mistake. So I knew it was about time for them to hook up if they hadn't already planned to do so.

I loved Roderick so much that I would overlook it. I was in denial that he was not going around her. But, in my heart of hearts, I knew that it was gonna be a problem. Besides, Roderick was too cool about everything. So, I just went on pretending that everything was OK. We would enjoy each other and just go through the dating/living together norms.

I began to have trouble with my little white car. It needed to be fixed because this morning when the girls and I went out to get in it for school and work; it would not start. I had a auto shop tow it. The auto man called me at work and told what the problem was with the car. They told me that it would cost about $1500 to fix it and it was not worth it for such an old car. I had been driving that car for about six years and I decided to get a new car. So I told Roderick where I had put up some money in the house for emergencies and for him to go and rent a car later, and pick me up at work. Then I would use the car while I go around town and look for a new car. He said that he would and then he would pick me up at work.

But guess what? He didn't! He ran off with my money and I didn't hear from him for about three days. I called his cell phone all day, every day, all day long. He finally answered. He said that he was upset because he had received a letter the same day denying his disability and that he needed to get away and be by his self. He claimed to have stayed in a hotel and that he drank, it all up. I didn't realize then that he had starting using drugs again. I was totally clueless and had no idea.

So, I said, "Well, you know that this changes things between us." I told him to come to the house and get his things.

But he didn't. He waited for about one week. Then all of a sudden, he showed up at my house with the police. I wasn't at home, my daughters were. I was out car hunting. I was in the middle of signing the loan papers. All of a sudden, my cell phone rang. I answered. It was Danielle explaining that he was there and he wanted his things. But ya know it wasn't that deep. He was a punk. He couldn't face me. So he needed the cops to protect him. He assumed that I was home and he really didn't know me. He wasn't sure how I would respond. So the girls let him get the stuff that was already packed.

Mind you- I wanted rid of him! So be gone! Besides, I was out purchasing my new wheels. I knew that he'd hear about it, and would be busted up because I had a new car. He wouldn't be able to drive it. So now you dogged my lil white car but look what I got, this time. I was sooo proud of myself. And I was sooo excited.

About two weeks later, I needed to replace a headlight. So I went to a local AutoZone to purchase them. I decided to go over to his cousin's Alicia's house and visit. Besides, I knew it would eventually get back to him about my new car. It would be a smack in the face. It was no doubt that he was staying with Rashida again down on Thirty-Fourth Street. So who cares? I'm going on with my life.

When I arrived at Alicia's House, which was just up the street from AutoZone, I was glad to see all his family we used to go and have drinks and party with. I promised Alicia that we would always keep in touch.

Alicia said, "You just missed him. He was just here about ten minutes ago. But, he said that he would be back."

I said, "Oh hell, it will trip him out to see that I have got a new car. And I can throw it up in his face."

Alicia and I continued to talk.

And sure enough he came back in and saying all along, "Whose Thunderbird is that?" And when he looked up, I was sitting there. He said, "Oh hell, what you doing here?"

I said, "Visiting."

He said, "You look good."

I said, "Hmmm," and I changed my conversations back over to Alicia.

He went into the back room.

It was good to see him. I was no longer mad at him, cause I don't hold grudges. I had started my new life anyways so what would it hurt to talk at him, not to him. So just then, one of my friends, walk in.

Alicia says, "Birdi, did you see Rhonda's new car? Girl, go and check it out."

And we winked at each other. It was killing him.

Everybody that came in asked whose Thunderbird was that out front.

Alicia confirmed that he was staying down on Thirty-Fourth Street with Rashida again.

I just shook my head and smiled as if he is a trip. And for someone to all ways have an open door to him. What is she about? She must be weak and have low self-esteem. Hmmm, she's stupid. Oh well, let her deal with him.

So Birdi and I took my car for a spin. We drove off and all the guys had made it outside and were looking at the car. So I felt special when I drove off.

Went to get some beer, and when I got back Roderick said, "I need to talk to you. We need to talk about what has happened. And I need to explain things to you."

We talked for about two hours in the kitchen all by ourselves.

When it was time for me to go, he had the nerve to ask me to give him a ride.

I said, "Where?" looking at him as if he was crazy.

He said, "Down on Thirty-Fourth Street."

I said, "Hell naw. I'm not gonna give you a ride to some girl's house. Yeah, right!"

He begged.

I said, "No," and I stuck to my word.

He kept looking at the clock.

I said, "Ya better get home before Rashida kicks ya ass. See, when you were living with me ya didn't have a curfew, just needed to not stay out overnight."

So he left, catching the bus. But I'm sure he'd see someone and get a ride. He knew everybody.

I stayed at Alicia's for about another hour, and then I left to go home. All the way home, I was thinking about all we had talked about. Then I thought to myself that he was a lot of fun. And he said that he's not happy at Rashida's house. He wanted me back.

So, I talked to him on the phone for about a week- everyday. We worked things out over the phone. So I took him back and told him to bring his things as well.

He said, "OK. I will have my brother-in-law, Ron, to go with me and help me get my things."

So, he did. About an hour later, he called and said, "She won't let me get my stuff. She started crying and shit and won't let me get my stuff."

So now me, being a woman, this became a competition thing. And I was gonna win. So I told him to call the police to meet him there so he could get his things, just like he tried to do with me.

So he did and she did her crying and everything, and begging him to stay.

I was standing outside and seen and heard it all. But I got even with her. I have him now and he left her for me. Sooo he must love me. So I thought. He came back home and for a while things were good.

Then he started staying out overnight again. Of course, he was over Rashida's house. So I continued to pretend that everything was OK. We continued to be with each other. As the months went by, we continued, as we were- him staying out on occasion, and me pretending that everything was A-OK. We continued to have a great time when things were all right. Things were OK for now.

Then one night after he had stayed out sorta late he came in and he knew that I was very angry with him, and after that night, we were married. The day that we got married, we went to my dad's house for our wedding celebration. It was lots of fun. The next day we're to be at his mom's for a cookout for the celebration of our marriage. I was excited and couldn't wait for all us to be together. We even had guests come from out of town for our wedding celebration.

Roderick and his brother-in-law, Ron went over to Roderick's sister, Glynnis's house. While they were there, Mom called looking for Roderick. She said Rashida was very upset to realize that we actually got married. She was upset that he would marry a girl that he's only known for a few years. He had known her for eleven. She was sooo upset that she had to leave work. So the family thought that he should give her a call and help to calm her down. So he did. But, his sister called and told me.

So, by the time he got to our house, I was hot. Out of all that we had been through with this Rashida stuff, how could he call and try to make her feel better? What was I- chop liver? I was soooo upset that I started cussing him out. He called me a B. Then it was on.

I said, "How can you talk to me that way? You just married me two days ago. And today I'm a B?" So I hauled off and hit him. I stole him in his jaw like I was a boxer.

He left and went to tell his mom like some big kid.

So, we ended up going to the celebration and being mad at each other. Both wishing we had never married the other. We both pretended that things were OK.

So the next morning was Sunday and we were to attend a church service for married couples. It was crazy knowing what all had happened just the day before, but I figured we needed pray to say the least. It was nice, and we both went on faking it.

Well, Monday was fine, but we were very quiet. Then Tuesday him and Chanielle got into a huge argument over something silly. So silly I can't even remember what it was about. I was asleep when the argument started. It all happened so fast. I ran into Chanielle's room to break up the argument, but he was choking her. My dog, Gigi, tried to protect Chanielle. Rockerick grabbed Gigi and threw her into the wall. That's how she broke her hip. Chanielle left that night to go stay with her dad.

Then Wednesday while I was at work, he moved all his things out of the house and went back to Rashida, down on Thirty-Fourth Street. This back and forth stuff just wouldn't stop. I was sooo devastated that I took me and the girls to stay with my grandfather. I needed to get out of the house. I stayed there for about a week.

But, then something came over me. I called his mom and told her to call him at Rashida's and tell him we needed to talk. He came over and we did. But, he was not ready to come home and deal with my daughter Chanielle, since the two of them didn't get along.

He said, "Rhonda, I love you. Just give me some time and I will be home. We need space."

So I said, "OK."

I knew that as soon as Rashida got on his nerves he'd be ready to come home. They could only stand each other for a short time. That's why they have been together sooo long, because they really never dealt with each other for long periods of time, just hit and misses.

So every night, I would imagine him and her being together in the same bed, and wondering if they were really having fun, the way we use too. It was sooo painful.

Everywhere I went; people congratulated me on my marriage. They had no idea three days after we were married that my husband abandoned me and my children to go back to his old, longtime girlfriend, Rashida. So I pretended that everything was fine, and went as if it was.

By now, I realized that he would play me and Rashida against each other. He'd tell me one thing and her, another. He had us hating that each other even existed.

So one day he called me at work from Rashida's house and professed his love to me. Then he asked to see me. Sooo me and my husband started sneaking around seeing each other. I was having an affair with my husband. How messed up is that? I would send him home to his girlfriend. For months, we did this.

He told me that he had promised her that he would stay with her until she had her foot surgery. So he and I continued to sneak and see each other. She only lives a few minutes from my house. I would spend time with him and then take him up the street and drop him off. We flirted with each other and we had sex with each other. Besides, he was my husband. So, Roderick and I would go to Carrollton-a little town outside of Louisville, for a getaway and have long drives in the country. Just like we did before we got married. We'd talk about working things out.

Then it came time for her surgery and he went with her and got her settled in. She was under lots of medication, so he would call me and we would talk on the phone. As the days went by, she would require him to spend more time helping her around the house and he was not going for it. So one morning he got dressed, fixed her something to eat, we met each other and he stayed all night with me. And he didn't even call her to say so. He just disappeared and moved back home.

Then we were together for about six months and enjoyed our time together.

He and Chanielle hardly got along at all. There were arguments one after another. I was miserable and so was he. But we somehow managed to stay together. Then we fell out again and he moved back into Rashida's house.

Then it was time for me to have a hysterectomy and I needed his help with the house. He said that he would work it out and go to the hospital with me. We knew that our marriage was over, but he would still help me through this. So the night of my surgery he stayed all night with me so we could get to the hospital at 5:00 am and get me settled in. I allowed him to keep my car so he could get back and forth to see me. I knew that he would be back and forth between me and Rashida but, I was sick and I didn't have time to care. I needed to focus on me and my surgery. I needed him to check in on the girls during the day. They didn't want to stay with family members because I would be home in two days so they would be OK. My family would check in on them while I was in the hospital. Danielle stayed home that day, but Chanielle went to school. I would see them later on that evening when my family and friends would come to visit. Sooo I felt OK with the arrangements.

Roderick loved attention. At the hospital, he would make a point to get noticed by the nurses and he was just loud. He always wanted to be the center of attention.

When they brought me out of recovery and was trying to get me adjusted in the bed, I asked my father for his hand to help me, not knowing that it would offend Roderick. But he was just looking for an excuse to leave anyways. So he left. He claimed to have had his feelings hurt because I didn't ask him to help me; I asked my father. Sooo whatever!

The day came for me to be released from the hospital. He called to see if I was ready. He came to get me.

As we pulled up to the house I said, "Oh I need to get my prescription filled."

He said, OK." So in the same breath he said, "I need twenty dollars."

I said, "I won't be able to give you money. I will be off work for the next six weeks and I just don't have it."

He got mad and left me in the car calling me names and said, "Find someone else to take you to get your medicine." He slammed the car door and walked on down the street.

I just got out of the car and walked slowly into the house, sat down and cried. I called my grandfather and he was not home. I called my sister and she was not answering her cell phone. But I needed my medication and I was not to drive until my six-week check-up. But when Danielle and Chanielle came home, I took them with me and drove to the store to get my medication. Then came home and got into the bed, and went to sleep.

My husband dogged me (treated me awful) during my surgery just like he did Rashida during her foot surgery. So we were even at least. He dogged us equally.

My first week home from the hospital was awful. All I did was take medicine and sleep.

The second week, the phone rings and it was Roderick apologizing. I let him come over. Rashida was at work during the day and he would spend time with me watching TV and helping me get around. There was no sex for at least six weeks so I felt safe. I knew that he was there because he wanted to be and not for sex. I had my surgery in January around the thirteenth. He visited me everyday for the next six weeks. Then on Valentine's Day, he stayed all night. From that point, he was home again.

One day, the phone rang and it was Rashida. She said that she was bringing Roderick his things and that she didn't want to have anything else to do with him. So she did and she said that she wished us the best and maybe I was the woman that would change him. She was through and I wouldn't have to worry about her ever being in our lives again. So after, she left, Roderick started going through his things and noticed that not all his things were there and he wanted to go back down to her house and make sure he got all his stuff. So we did. When we got there; she let us both in.

Before ya knew it, we were all sitting down having a drink and talking about everything. So Roderick and I left and went home. I felt like the Rashida-Roderick thing was finally over and now we could work on our marriage.

Rashida wanted him to get a divorce and he didn't want one, and neither did I. So I thought to myself, now we can work on our marriage.

So I thought, until Shaquana came into our lives.

MY HYSTERECTOMY

My recovery is going slow.

But well, the pain that I'm going through is nothing compared to the pain of having my heart ripped out by my husband.

My gas pains are equal to my heart pain and palpations.

My stomach cramps are equal to the pain of him beating me one night in my arms, back and shoulders.

When I cannot make it to the bathroom fast enough and my bladder is full, it is equal to the fullness I had for him in my heart.

Not being able to raise myself up and get out of bed in one motion is like his foot being at the base of my throat. That is what I felt when he stole money from me, even after I had already given him some.

The nights of diarrhea is equal to the nights I waited for him to come home while having my new car out partying,

The bloating and swollen belly is equal to all the times that he called me fat and told me I needed to lose weight.

The stitches are equal to every time we broke up and I tried to heal. But, every time he came back too fast to allow me to move on with my life.

The sleepless nights are equal to my visualizing him with Rashida and wondering if they were having fun like we did.

The different positions I would try to get in to be comfortable or to fall asleep were equal to all the ways I tried to make our marriage work. I tried everything!

Trying to bend over and not being able to touch the ground is equal to my self-esteem level- about an inch off the ground.

My being broke with no cash is equal to the times we were together and he drained me financially because he wouldn't help me out.

My being scared of not healing properly is equal to the abuse that I allowed towards my children. What damage it may have caused them, only time will tell.

Being lonely is equal to him being in someone else's home and not ours.

My trying to put my sweat pants on and getting my foot all tangled up, as I struggle to keep my balance is equal to him making me feel all confused and twisted in the mind- all of his brainwashing and manipulation.

The times that I would try and walk through the house for exercise and would lose my balance were equal to the nights I drank so much I would be drunk so I could feel no pain. Trying to drink my sorrows away.

When I would try to stand up, it would take time to get into a position that I was secure in enough to try and take a few steps is equal to all the times I took the first step to starting my new life without him by putting him out, only to take him back.

The times that I would almost fall for no reason was equal to the times that I felt lightheaded at work, from not eating because I had no money because I had given him my last the night before for drugs.

Gone,

Uterus- Our marriage

Fallopian tubes- My daughters losing respect for me

Ovaries- No more calling me names

Fibroid tumors- Him never being able to hurt me again

CARROLLTON

Tonight would be special. It's Friday and we have the house to ourselves. The girls are away for the weekend. We have decided to spend the evening by the fireplace. Usually when we spend time in the living room, we play all our favorite CD's and have drinks, laugh, talk, and just enjoy ourselves. We had everything we needed: our beer, cigarettes, liquor and he had his drug of choice (crack). So, tonight was going to be perfect. I will fix a special meal for us: spaghetti and sauce, garlic bread and Caesar salad with ranch dressing.

I'm looking forward to an evening with my husband and I can't wait to get off of work. Roderick and I have talked on the phone several times today. We both are looking forward to an evening alone with no interruptions. So hurry up 4:00 and come on!

After I got in the house, I began to prepare supper. I showered and relaxed after a long week at work. Roderick was in the bedroom watching television. Our relationship was going well in spite of all the things that had been going on. Our relationship had many downs and it was nice when we would get together and enjoy each other's company. This was different from when we dated. We weren't together all the time. But now, we're together 24/7. Sometimes we'd get on each other's nerves. Roderick had been doing some work around the house like: painting, cleaning out the cellar and just doing some of the things that I really needed him to do. I was finally happy. Usually he will half do a job and never complete it. Now Roderick was different. When he was high, he would be more energetic. Believe it or not, he'd be more focused. So I was happy and he was happy. We were on the same page and it was nice to be that way.

After supper, we went into the living room. Our bedroom and living room are adjacent. So, sometimes we would open the sliding double-wood doors. It looked as if we had this huge bedroom, almost like a suite. I love it that way. We sat down and began to talk and laugh. I finally had a chance to relax.

Our latest argument was about, the girls. The fact that they were spoiled and that I catered to them. He never once mentioned the catering that I do for him. We had been at each other like cats and dogs. So, I welcomed this change of peace.

Roderick asked me if he could have this dance. I said, "Yes." To me, we danced like Fred Astaire and Ginger Rogers. He was sooo smooth on his feet. He took time to show me how to flow. And over the months I could dance as well as he could. So, dancing to us was lots of fun. I loved it when he would hold me. I was like a teenager- feeling puppy love feelings: my palms would sweat, my heart would beat fast and I would have that queasy feeling in my stomach. Just silly in love, so much, that I cannot explain. As the night went on, we began to watch a few movies and just really enjoy our time together.

It was about eleven o'clock. Roderick had run out of Crack. He wanted to run out and get some more. Well I was too relaxed and I said for him to go ahead. He knew that he couldn't drive the car from previous fallouts we have had with him not coming back at a decent hour, being disrespectful to the fact that it was my car and I could choose when I would allow him and when I would not. So he was cool with it.

He said," I'm just going around the corner and see what I can find."

Well I knew that it was not an issue because lots of people sell crack. It's almost on every corner. You'd be surprised where it exchanges hands at: grocery stores, restaurant parking lots, schools, parks, and neighborhood playgrounds. So I knew that he'd find what he was looking for.

Our rule of thumb was to always kiss each other goodbye because ya never know if it would be our last time seeing each other. So he gave me a big kiss and went out the back door of the house. He'd go that way for a short cut over to the other streets. So I anticipated his return. So I went into the kitchen, got some more ice, and fixed me another drink. I sat back into the living room, listened to the music, and just continued to relax.

After about say twenty minutes or so, I began to wonder. Who has Roderick ran into? He is a talker and meets no strangers. So I assumed that he was held up in a conversation. It was always someone from back in the day (years ago). So I decided to watch TV for a while as I sat and waited for him. And sure enough he came back. I'd say about an hour after that. So of course I was angry and not in the mood for romance by now. I hate how he just dismisses everyone or anything, for that crack. He could care less about you and anyone else. I hate how he lets it control him.

So I sat angry with my face all turned up, as he explained why he was gone sooo long. Now he started out by saying that he went to purchase some crack from ya boy, around the way and he didn't have any. So, he told me to go and ask ya girl, so Roderick claims that he went to some girl's house name Shaquana. He had not known her before. When he knocked on the door and asked if anyone had it, she invited him in and she did have some. They sat down and began to laugh and talk. She only had a bit and asked if he would ride with her to purchase some more. He said he would but he needed to get back to his wife (yeah right?). He was probably all over her. Well he went on to say that Shaquana tried to entice him after they got back. While he was smoking, she went into the other room and came back with something more revealing on. He claims that he never touched her.

Now if he thought the mood was killed earlier, it truly was now. As I sat trying to act as if I could care less, he was actually bragging about how proud of his self he was for not hitting it (not having sex with her) and he was truly dedicated to our marriage. I thought to myself- hmmm, what is this leading too? And he could see it in my face, how upset I was, and how he had ruined a good weekend. Forget the night! I didn't want him to touch me.

So he spent the rest of the night talking about himself as usual. I would just sit and listen. The one good thing about him was sex. And hell, it was the weekend. He wanted me and I wanted him. I figured that if he had been with this Shaquana girl, he wouldn't be able to perform. I had worked hard all week. I deserved to enjoy myself and have a good weekend. So I was going to let it go just like I had been doing all the other stuff. Why would this be different? So I just wanted to have sex with him and move on. At this point, who cares? I deserve to enjoy myself. As much stuff as I have went through- and so why not? Besides, he was my husband. The next day we would be at each other's throats, so let's get it on!!!

As usual, it was great. Roderick really knew what he was doing in the bedroom. It was ecstasy. I was able to relax and have a great evening after all. The weekend was fine. We actually had a decent one. No bouts with the girls and no arguments over things. Things were actually going well. And even when I would call home to talk to him from work; he actually had a conversation. It was good for things to be looking up for us. Maybe, just maybe, he was starting to settle into this marriage thing. And maybe, just maybe, he was going to do right!

Monday night football, the Jets are playing. I love the Jets and his favorite team is the Steelers. So, we would always make bets as to whose team was going to win. That was another part of our fun- the football and basketball games. Roderick was quiet though, which was unusual for him. I didn't think anything of it, just a nice quiet evening at home with my husband. I like the sound of that.

The next morning when I was leaving for work, I did the usual. I divided up the cigarettes whoever of us was low, because I could get some on my way to work. He usually wouldn't leave out till about ten o'clock or so. I gave him a kiss on the forehead on my way out the door. We said our, "I love you's." But, something wasn't right and I could feel it- woman's intuition I guess. So, I called home as soon as I sat down at my desk and he answered and he sounded sad. But, Roderick had bouts with depression. He was bi-polar and he was on crack, coupled with all the prescription medications for heart problems, and arthritis and high blood pressure. Sooo I just assumed that was the problem. He sounded OK.

So, I said, "Honey, I was just thinking about you. Sooo, I called."

He said, "OK. I'm going back to bed."

His highs and lows would come and go. If I didn't watch myself, my moods would change as his did. And that was not fair to me. So I would constantly try to lift my own spirits with music and reading the Bible. That's what keeps me sane- a natural high.

I was with the man that I chose, in spite of all his shortcomings. I loved him and would try to help him any way that I could. At work, I would look up the names of his medications and try to see if I could help him deal with his side effects. I wanted to support him anyway that I could. I would encourage him to stop using drugs. I even offered to go to counseling with him to continue my support. I would encourage him to go to church for some spiritual uplifting. I would encourage him through my love and determination that I had for our marriage and the love that I had for him. There wasn't anything that I wouldn't do to help him over come all of his bondage.

So we hung up saying we'd see each other later. Throughout the day, I kept feeling something was not right. But I went on and had a good day. When I arrived to the house, he was there, but he acted like he was guilty for something. So I just played as if I had not noticed his mood and went on as if everything was OK. During our conversations throughout the evening I noticed that he kept on saying that when he gets his disability check, that he was going to Carrollton to go and do some fishing.

Carrollton is a small town, about forty minutes outside of Louisville, Kentucky. He would go there for the summers as kid. He always referred to it as a getaway. When we first started dating, we'd go to Carrollton and have a great time. We'd have cookouts with friends, have an annual Fourth of July swim party and we'd go to the clubs and dance. Carrollton would put you in the mind of Mayberry on TV where Aunt Bee, Opie, and Andy Griffith took place. It's a nice, quiet and settled town- a place to go clear your mind. Over the years, we must have made hundreds of trips there just to get away from the city.

So, when he kept saying he wanted to go to Carrollton, I said, "OK that would be nice for you."

But he always said, "Oh, I'd be home before you get off of work."

So, I would just smile.

As the week went on, I started noticing how he was beginning to become distant, not in conversation, but in our "family business". He was not interested in who had called, what bills were due and he didn't even mention anything about the girls getting on his nerves. He was in his own world. He never complained about what was for dinner or if the house didn't pass his inspection of being neat and clean. He wasn't himself- the way I had grown to know him.

So I asked what was up with him.

He said, "Oh, nothing." But, he had the look of having a secret on his face.

Then one night we were having dinner. He brought up the subject of "Hey, remember when I told you, back in the day, how the girls would flock to see and be with me?"

And I laughed and said, "Oh you mean one hundred years ago? When you were the big football player?"

He smiled and said, "Yes."

I laughed and said, "Ya, what about it?"

He said, "Watch this", picked up the phone off the base, and dialed a number. I heard a female's voice.

I looked at him, motioned, and said in a whisper, "Who is that?" With my face all tore up, a look of curiosity on my face, and my eyebrows up, and he had that same look on his face, as if he was keeping a secret again.

He was telling the person on the other end that he was sitting and enjoying the evening with his wife. When he didn't tell me who it was, I got up and started picking up our plates from supper to take back into the kitchen. Then I heard him say that he was going to go and make love to his wife. So I stopped in my tracks, thinking who in the world is he taking to? So he hung up after a brief conversation. I was standing over him when he hung up and just looked like who was that.

He laughed and said, "I still got it."

I said, "Got what?" Thinking in my mind, you dumb fool. I know you didn't do what I just think you did.

He said, "That was this girl who gave me her phone number and I'm gonna play her like a fool."

I said, "WHAT!!!"

He said, "Rhonda, she wants me and I can get money from her. And just use her for whatever we need."

I politely, walked closer to him and said, "You make me sick."

By then, all my dinner had come back up and I threw up all over him. I showered and went to bed. I didn't even have the energy to argue with him. He was disgusting. I knew that he was sick in the head. And I was too, to continue this type of abuse. I mean right in your face abuse and disrespect, just down right disgust.

The next day we were back to not speaking again. And this time I went to sleep on the couch. Damn, we had just got over a big breakup months before and had only been back together now for about two months because of some other dumb stuff. That's all we did: breakup, makeup, breakup and makeup. Sooo, here we go again. This time we went longer without speaking. I spent my time in the living room; and he in the bedroom. I went my way; and he went his. No one was cooking; and no one was ever at home. That went on for a few weeks.

Then one day when I came in he said, "Rhonda, your auntie called. They said for you to come right over. Your brother had gotten beaten up by some guys and he was hurt bad. They had called an ambulance."

So I turned to go back out the door, and he said, "Do you want me to drive?"

I said, "Yes," with tears in my eyes. I was thinking to myself that this was the phone call that we have all expected to get. The only difference is that I thought it would be in the wee hours of the morning.

My brother is an alcoholic and is always in some fight or altercation. Some are worse than others; but this sounded pretty bad. So the ride over, I was crying and thinking all the thoughts of my brother and I as kids and praying that the Lord would spare him just once more. And that if the Lord did, I would do what I could to include my brother in my life more. This was really hard to do, because when he would get drunk he'd call me all sorts of names. And that was hard to take. So I was very cautious as to having him come to house and be around me and the girls.

As we arrived at the scene, the ambulance was pulling off and one of my aunts said, "He's bad off. You might want to go on and see about him." And she told me that my dad would be on up and they all would as well. So, we got back into the car, and headed to the hospital.

And sure enough, it was bad. Upon entering the hospital, we asked to see him. We were instructed to meet with the rest of the family in the chapel. So it doesn't take a "rocket scientist to know that if we were all to meet in the chapel" that it was not good news. And it wasn't. He was in a semi-comma state and heavily sedated. The next few hours would be crucial. So, while there, I just keep giving Roderick really nasty looks. I wouldn't sit by him or hardly talk- only when necessary. So we stayed as long as any of us could and then we prayed and put him in God's hands. The majority of us had to go to work the next morning and there was nothing we could do but wait. Sooo, my dad and granddad stayed the night to look after my brother.

When we got home, Roderick apologized and said he was sorry for what had happened to my brother and he was sorry for calling the girl on the phone.

I said, "Oh OK." He hugged and kissed me and held me in his arms as I tried to fall asleep.

The next day at work my father called and gave us the good news and said my brother would be OK. He could have visitors. So after work, Roderick, the girls and I headed for the hospital. While we sat and visited, I just looked at Roderick strut around like everything was OK. I still really had little to say, but I pretended that everything was OK as usual in front of my family. They had heard sooo many things from me about Roderick that I started sparing them the details. It was useless. I just didn't have it in me anymore to say one way or another how things were going on in my home. Roderick also pretended that things were all right and the days passed. But, I knew that I needed to leave him alone for good. I just didn't know how.

So one day, I called home from work. Feeling that feeling, that something was wrong again. The girls had just got home from school and I asked, "Is Roderick there?"

They said, "No."

I said, "Hmm, Danielle, check and see if anything of his clothes are missing or out of place."

She said, "OK, hold on." She came back to the phone and said, "Momma, all of his stuff is gone: his clothes, shoes, books, music-everything is gone."

So I just said in a soft breath, "OK, I'll be home soon."

She said, "OK."

So when I hung up the phone at my desk, my hands, started trembling, and I knew that he was not coming to pick me up from work. So I asked a co-worker, Nadeen, to give me ride home.

That morning, I had let him take me to work because he was to get one of the back checks from disability and he and I was going to go around and pay some bills. But I had in my mind that as soon as he would pay the bills I would put him out, but it looks like he had already outsmarted me again and had another plan. All day long I had called the house to see if he was there, but no answer. I called his mother and she said that he got the check and left with Mr. Franklin, a dear friend of ours, and a father figure to Roderick. So I felt somewhat OK. I knew that Mr. Franklin would have him take care of the rent that was owed, "back rent" due. Mr. Franklin was also our landlord. The two of them were like "Sanford and Son". They would hang out together and have lunch. Roderick would make extra money to make ends meet. So I was pretty certain that he would take care of that bill. The other bills were in question. I couldn't take off of work. Sooo I had to let happen what would.

Around 3:00, he called me at work saying that he would be late picking me up and that he was over in Indiana. I knew from his conversation that he had already been using and that the drama would soon begin. After about twenty minutes passed, I just knew that he wasn't coming to pick me up. It had happened sooo many other times that I could just sense that this was one of those times. So within the next twenty minutes, I must have called home about ten times looking for him and asking the girls if they had seen him yet. And to no avail.

Sooo, after Nadeen drove me home; I went into the house and I started making call after call. Then I decided to call Mr. Franklin to see if Roderick had told him where he was going.

Mr. Franklin said, "He told me that he had a special evening planned for the both of you. And that he seemed to be excited."

So I said, “What about the money?”

Mr. Franklin said, "He paid me the back rent. He paid me a total of $2663.72- all that he owed me.”

So I was relieved. Now, his check was to be $4700. We were going to pay the other bills and try to get my car fixed from the wreck. Mr. Franklin had allowed us to pay him later since we were having such a hard time. Mr. Franklin knew that when the money would arrive, he'd see to it that he got his part. Mr. & Mrs. Franklin have been sooo nice to me and the girls. They have helped us time after time. They have truly been a blessing to us.

Now where the hell is Roderick? And where is my car? Of all nights, he would have it. Tonight is Danielle's Junior Prom and I need my car to get her to the restaurant where the Prom will be. I pretended to be calm in front of the girls. Besides, tonight is Danielle's night. I was sooo upset. I cannot begin to tell you my feelings. All I know is that he's a sorry dog and he needs to be stopped from doing crazy things like this.

The evening was getting later and later, and closer and closer to the time for Danielle to go to the prom. So I asked my brother-in-law, Marcus- Roderick's little brother if he would take her. I didn't want to impose any further, because the family was sooo tired of hearing all the bad things that Roderick was doing to me and my kids. So I told him that I would see to her getting home if he could just get her there I would truly appreciate it. Roderick was always jealous of me and Marcus's relationship.

See, Marcus used to date my sister. And Marcus and I began to be friends and talk on the phone years before Roderick and I got married. Even when Roderick and I would break up, Marcus and I would still keep in touch and call each other daily. He was like a brother to me and Roderick couldn't stand it.

So Marcus came and escorted her, just as if he was her date for the night. I didn't even have money for a throw away camera. Roderick knew that tonight was to be special for us and I think he did this on purpose. He was sooo jealous of my girls. Just like a kid, he wanted all the attention and all the spot light.

Where the hell is he and my CAR???

I laid down after Danielle left and feel asleep. I couldn't even cry. I had been sooo used to being hurt and disappointed, that it had become the norm for me. I just tried to sleep the evening away. YAWN!!! OH!!! It's almost 1:30 am. Danielle should be getting home soon. I had told her to call herself a cab if she was unable to get a ride home with a friend and then I would pay her back the money next week when I got paid.

That's a shame. My daughter had to catch a cab on prom night. And on top of that, she had to pay for it. I'm such a mess up as a mother. I hate myself. I'm so stupid. There, I said it. Yes, I'm sooo stupid.

As I began to lie back down, watching the clock, I thought to myself. She should be coming in very soon. Not even ten minutes later, she arrived. I went to the door, because I had heard a car door shut and there she was. It was like Cinderella turning into a pumpkin, and having to come home in a cab. I was sooo sad. But I had to pretend to Danielle that everything was all right.

Her first words were, “Did he bring the car back?”

And my first words to her were, “Did you have a good time?”

I sat with Danielle and we talked about the fun that she had. She showed me pictures of her friends and she went on to bed.

By now, it was about 2:30 am and still no car, no phone call and no Roderick. So I then went back to bed and somehow fell asleep. RING. RING. RING, it was my mother-in-law calling. I could see it on the Caller ID. It was now Saturday morning.

She said, “Have you heard from him? Marcus told me what happened.”

I went over all that I knew and she told me all that she knew. He had come over early that morning, and she hadn't seen him since. So we both were at a stand still. We both agreed that he had been doing good and that it seemed as if he was trying this time to do what was right. But, there were some things I that I had not told her that he had done, just to save face.

All day, I waited and watched and waited and watched. Every time I heard a car door or even what sounded like one and I'd go back and forth and back and forth, until I just gave up. So then, I decided to call the jail, and the hospitals. No one had anyone by that name. Night had fallen and I went to bed. I prayed all through the night. Every time I would roll over or turn my pillow over, I would pray and ask God to give me the strength to make it through this one.

I said the same things. “If you let me get my car back, this time I promise I would not let him drive it again.” But while I was praying I was also saying in my head, you know that you will, you always do. So stop lying to yourself and God. Because he knows already that you will. So I felt that my prayers were just empty ones.

At this point, it was obvious that he was gone on a crack binge. But why did he take his clothes? All of a sudden I thought to myself-Carrollton!!! But I didn't react on it. I had some friends there but it would take me some going through some of my papers to look up there telephone numbers. So I just let it go for the moment and I decided to just watch some TV and try relaxing a bit.

I knew that I was not going to let the devil stop me from going to church. So when I woke up it was Sunday morning and I started getting dressed and told the girls to also. So I called my dad’s cell number and he had it off because he was in Sunday school. So then, I called my cousin Kyrie for a ride. This morning of all mornings, she was sleeping in. Then I called my other cousin and she was gone already. So I was sooo frustrated that I told the girls just forget it, we’re staying home. I said, “The Lord knows my heart!!!” So I watched one of the church evangel shows on TV, and I prayed and asked God to help me, to help myself.

Well it was now Sunday night and no news yet. So I began to prepare for bed and work for the next morning.

When I got up I decided to call a cab for work and the girls walked to the bus stop. I went on to work as if nothing had happened. Throughout the day, I must have made a million phone calls, checking and talking to old friends. I was trying to see if anyone had seen Roderick, or even heard from him. And to no avail. After work, I went home and sat and sat and prayed and prayed and waited and waited and waited.

Tuesday, I started the same routine. But this time I decided to set a trap for Roderick. I knew that he would come back while we were gone to work and school. So I left the phone off the hook, and I would just call all day on and off, to see if it was a busy signal or if it would ring. If it would ring then I'd at least know that he had been in the house. And sure enough, I called after about the fiftieth time, and it was not busy.

It rang and he had the nerve to answer and as if nothing had happened. I told him, "Whatever you are doing and whatever you decide to do, I don’t care, but if you don't leave my car, I will have you arrested for stealing the car. So, leave the keys on my bed and get out of my life.”

We hung up. So I couldn’t wait for my girls to get home to see if he had in fact left my car like I said. They finally came home, called me at work, and said that he left the car but no keys. At first, I was angry, but forget it. I'll pay a locksmith to change the locks on the car and the house. So, I was just glad that my car was back. So I asked Nadeen to give me a ride home.

When I arrived there she sat, my green, Ford Thunderbird. Even though it had been wrecked last year, it was still my car. So I opened it and their lay my keys on the seat. I was able to get in without keys by using a code on the touch pad on the side of the door.

When Roderick and I had talked, I was sooo into if he was going to leave my car that I forgot all about what he was rambling on about. Something like he had bought him a house in the country and that when he gets it fixed up, I could come and visit with him. And that he knew that he was wrong; and that he was sorry. As I began to explain to Nadeen what he was saying, she and I both just shook our heads. We tried to figure out just what was going on his head. And what in the world was he doing? So, she and I sat for a while and then she left.

I just laid down. I was sooo tired from all the drama of the last five days. I just needed to relax. I got up to take a shower, took two sleeping pills and went back to bed.

The next day, I was sooo overwhelmed over his actions that I finally decided to call my girlfriend and her boyfriend that actually lived in Carrollton, Kelly Jo and Chester.

"Hey, Kelly Jo. This is Rhonda from Louisville."

“Oh, hi girl. Hey, what’s been going on?”

“Well…I was wondering if you had seen Roderick lately?”

"Yeah. He came here last week driving your car with some girl saying that you and he had broken up but you all were the best of friends. And that's how he had your car. He and the girl are renting a house from me up the road. I guess they go together or something.”

“Hum…well, it's like this. He stole my car for about five days. He left the house with all his clothes. He just said that he was wrong but he had to do it.”

"OH hell girl! Leave him alone! Have ya had enough yet? Rhonda, you deserve sooo much better.”

“Well thanks. I gotta go. But, I will call back because I want more details as to what went on and what is going on."

“OK. Call me anytime.”

“OK. Thank you. Talk to you later.”

“OK. Bye."

So I immediately hung up from talking to Kelly Jo, called Roderick’s daughter, and told her what was going on. She was not the least bit shocked.

Her words were, "That's my daddy

I was just in awe. I had heard stories from other family members and Roderick himself. But I never knew that he was sooo childish. And with bi-polar and schizophrenia, there’s no telling why he made such a move. He does things on a whim- without thinking of the consequences, and the ramifications. He doesn’t care what or who it will effect at that time. Whether it's his illness, crack cocaine or him just being a nasty person. He still needs to take responsibility and be responsible. He can’t or better still, he just won’t.

I couldn’t wait to talk to Kelly Jo again. Cause I still cannot believe my ears. He actually packed up all his clothes, abandoned his wife, and ran off to another town with another woman. And moved to Carrollton- of all places to start a new life! Now ain't that a trip! This is Jerry Springer stuff!!! A wife mind you, that will do anything for him and that has given him chance after chance after chance. And this is the thanks I get for being in love with him? Damn! This is cut throat stuff. This time he went for the jugular vein. He's literally trying to kill me!!!

Well right now, I must just take things for what is what and move on with my life. I cannot believe this. I did everything for him. I have tried all that I know to make things right. But I cannot help but to think if it was something I did. How messed up is that? He does whatever he wants to and I feel guilty. Maybe it's because he was bored with the sex. And maybe if I had just been a little more free to explore things. Or could it be because he found that he was not in love with me anymore. I just sat and began to go over things more and more. Trying to figure out what was going on in his head- and why he'd do such things. Hmmm, it was just a few days ago that he had left all these love notes all around the house saying, "I love you," and "You are the best," and "The woman I love," so, why this, and why now? What was going on with him? Where did he meet this girl? Who was she? How long have they known each other? What made him pack up and move? Questions, questions, questions!

The only person who could answer some of these questions would be Kelly Jo. So I called her. "Hey girl. Whatz up?"

"Oh, nothing. Just watching TV."

"Well, hell. I called to see if I could get some information on my husband and the floozy that he ran off with."

She began to tell me what was up. She said that they had been in Carrollton for about one week. They look like that happy couple sometimes. She said that some days he would look like he had the world on his shoulders and that he was really not happy. This girl was going around saying that they were engaged to be married. But everyone knows better. So what in the hell is she talking about?

"Girl, ya lying."

"No."

"OK. OK. Um, who is she?"

"Well, she said her name is Shaquana."

"And what the hell does she look like?"

"She's about 5'6" or so and she's sorta big, not too big. She wears a weave ponytail and it just bounces around. But she seems like she's OK. I can't really get into her because ya know ya my girl Rhonda and I just ain't feeling her. And his ass is full of bull, talking about ya'll being the best of friends. Rhonda, leave him alone."

And in a quite mousey voice I say, "I know, and I will." But, my heart wouldn't allow me and knew it, because I was too hooked. Some of the attractiveness to him was how spontaneous he was and how he'd do spur of the moment things- never a dull moment. But this was bad. This hurt me really bad. I don't know about getting through this one.

Kelly Jo went on saying that the house they were renting was not ready yet. They had stayed in a hotel some nights and slept in my car at the trailer park the other nights.

I said, "You lying!"

She said, "Hell naw. I'm not!"

So we ended the conversation by saying that we would keep in touch, we would get together before the summer was out, and we loved each other and to take care. She assured me that he was not happy and that he was just going through the motions.

So after we hung up, I sat on the side of the bed and just cried and cried and cried.

RING! RING! RING!!! I looked at the Caller ID and it was my mother-in-law calling again to check on me and to see if I had heard anything else. So I gave her the update and she and I hung up. She said that she was praying for us and for me to do the same.

Once again, I needed to evaluate things and I knew all this was bull. But, I still loved him- even if he didn't me. And too me, he was my best friend. So, I'd be losing my best friend and that would be hard to do. For the last three years, I had made him be my best friend in my mind. I knew that not only was he my best friend; he was my lover and he was my partner. I was "ADDICTED TO HIM LIKE HE WAS TO CRACK COCAINE!" I still needed to talk to him. I needed to hear his voice. And I wanted to hear out of his mouth what was really going on. The reason I knew that it was an addiction was because I couldn't leave him alone. I had to have him.

I had put sooo much time and energy into him- trying to fix him and make him RIGHT- that I couldn't stop now. I knew that I had tried this and that, but still there was something that I could do. I know in his own way he loves me. I know he does. I'm trying to convince myself.

What about all of our good times and the fun things that we have done? Speaking of fun, I loved to go to Carrollton. It was a getaway for me too. It was Saturday night. We'd paint the Carrollton red. It was dinner and dancing. We looked so good together. We partied at the "Landing", a club right on the river's edge. It was so nice and romantic. Roderick was such a gentleman that night. I had never been to the landing before. So, he escorted me to the ladies room. I had to go badly, but there was a line about twenty ladies deep. So I knew it would be impossible to wait. So Roderick put on his charm and before you knew it they let me go ahead of them all. It won my heart. I felt like a princess that night! Roderick was in rare form.

I have always wanted to live in a small town where everybody knows everybody. Just like one big neighborhood. So I always was game for the ride and the getaway, but he has turned something special into something nasty. I couldn't believe of all places he'd go. Why Carrollton!?!

Oh God, I love him sooo! Please, help us to work things out. And please let him come to his senses. And please let him know that I think about him daily. Oh God, help me! I miss him. I miss his touch. I miss his smile. I miss our fun nights. I miss being married to him. I need him. What was I to do?

WAIT! What is wrong with me? Hell naw. I must be crazy and stupid. Lord, help me to help myself. As the day went on I would do the normal things: like watch TV, talk on the phone, clean house and go walking; trying to stay focused but it was almost impossible. I was drawn to the memories of us. All the late nights, we stayed up and talked. I was drawn in like a vacuum.

And no one could begin to understand. I had lots of support from friends and family. Everyone wanted me snap out of if it. But I knew that I was in tooo deep to turn back now. He was gonna love me and my girls and this was gonna work. It had to or I would just die. I had put all my hopes and dreams into him and our marriage. This was my project. I had never worked so hard on anything in my life. I had to be successful; otherwise, I'd be a failure to me and the world. I wanted to take a man that was considered nothing to the world and make him something special. I wanted the glory and I wanted the fame as being the woman that fixed him and helped him to change his life around. And I could reap the benefits of the whole thing, so I must not stop. He was gonna love me. I'm staying. I ain't going just like the song by Jennifer Holiday. He was gonna love me!!! Besides, what man in his right mind would have me now? I was used up sexually, mentally, emotionally, and financially- and I was "WHOOPED". Used baggage- who would want someone like that? I wouldn't be any good to another man because my heart and soul was into Roderick. I loved him from the bottom of my soul however deep that is. I just know it is at the point of no return.

God, please forgive me for putting someone before you. I know that Roderick is like a god to me. Please forgive me for losing my focus and for allowing myself to be sooo weak. And Father, forgive me for not doing good in your sight. Father, forgive me for all of my sins. And help me to help myself!!! And I laid my head down and went to bed.

The next day it was off to work. The usual routine with me and the girls doing mother and daughter things: the movies, the mall and walking in the park with our dog, Gigi.

But, in my mind, I needed to do something. And I need to do it quick before this girl could really hook him. So, I called Kelly Jo again to see what I could find out.

She said, "Oh girl, he's here. He's here. He just came over to see me and Chester. To see if we had some charcoal so he could grill out."

My hands started to sweat, my heart started racing and my mouth was dry. I tried to swallow, but I couldn't.

She said in a soft voice, "Ya wanna talk to him?"

I said, "Yes."

So she called him to the phone. "Hey, Roderick. Someone wants to talk to you." I heard him asking, "Who is it?"

He answered, "Hello?"

And I took a deep breath and said, "Hello, Mr. Davis."

He said, "Rhonda, what's wrong?"

He figured that it had to be something wrong because he knew that he had devastated me sooo with this last blow that there is no way I'd be calling him.

I said, "Nothing. I needed to talk to you and hear your voice."

We talked for about half of an hour. He kept on apologizing. I told him that he was not a man. That he could have told me this before doing all of this. He said, that he wanted to, but the day that he was going to pack his things, I had left him a note saying how much I loved him on the mirror and it messed him up. He knew that he had this planned and he couldn't get up enough nerves to tell me so he just left. I said the next time you decide to run, take your own car and not steal someone else's. He just laughed as if he knew that part was messed up too- stealing the car and especially having some slut in it.

"So, what have you been doing?"

I said, “Walking, doing some writing and trying to take all of this in. What are you going to do? And how long are you planning on staying? Like for the rest of your life? Or, what is going on? And who is this girl your with? Roderick, I know everything. What are you doing? We just got married!!!”

“Rhonda, I needed to get away. I needed to find out what I wanted. And being a husband is OK. But me and your girls- I just can’t do the father thing again.”

“Oh, hell naw! You weren’t a father to your kids either. And you cheated on Yasmin, your first wife too. Roderick, when will you take life serious and stop ruining things and playing around?”

And there was dead silence on the other end of the phone for a few seconds. Then he said in a convincing voice, "Rhonda, I really do love you. Just give me some time and space for a while. I’m getting it together.”

“OK. Well, what do I do in the meantime, sit and twiddle my thumbs? While you, continue to play house with ole girl and ya know I have needs and wants? So, now what?”

He said, “I know. Well, I will be in town in a few days. We can talk then.”

So we told each other that we loved each other and hung up.

And I hung my head in shame, as usual. Why am I sooo trapped? Why won’t I allow myself to get out? What is going on? I must have had a stroke or something and have literally lost my mind. I was madly in love, trapped, and addicted. It was like being on a roller coaster ride. I wanted off, but at the same time, I was enjoying the ride as long as we were together. I was GONE off on him. I was addicted!!!! The thought of another woman is just unreal. I thought he loved me and me only. Why would he tell me so? What about our friends and family? They all loved seeing us together. When things were right between us, we even looked good! Together, we used to get compliments from everyone telling us how happy we looked together. My heart was aching. I needed my husband.

Roderick never did come home like he said. But, we continued talking to each other on the phone. He would call me every night and we would talk. Not sure where ole girl was. I guess he was calling from someone’s home or something, maybe a phone booth, who knows. After about a month of our talking and never seeing each other, I decided to move on, and let things be the way they were. So I tried not to think about him. I just focused on me, my walking, my reading and writing and going to church. I could tell by our conversations that he wasn't happy and he admitted himself.

Now, what he was doing or trying to achieve was unknown to me. About a month later, I was going over to Roderick's mother's house. Just as I turned the doorknob to enter, an old friend was coming up the walkway, and he told me that Mr. Franklin was in the hospital. He needed to have surgery. Well, everyone was put out with Roderick, due to his disappearing act. But, they knew how much we cared about the Franklin's. So, I told Roderick's mother that I will call and leave a message for Roderick and I did.

That same weekend, Roderick came home to check on his old buddy. When he arrived on this end of town, he called me and we met at mom's house- his mother. At first, he couldn't believe his eyes. I had lost about forty pounds since we had seen each other. I know that I looked good. Sooo did he. We hugged each other, but he motioned to kiss me and I pulled back.

"Where is your friend? The slut you ran off with?"

He said that she was visiting her family also."

"Here in Louisville? She from Louisville?"

And he dropped his head as if he had some shame, but I question his morals and values.

He said, "Yes. Sit down, Babe, and let me tell you everything. Remember the night that I was late coming back and said that I had met a girl who tried to seduce me but I turned her away? And remember the day I called a girl in front of your face? Well…that is Shaquana."

"Shaquana, she lives from around the corner from your grandfather?" Your ass is crazy!"

"Oh uh uh. Her daughter lives there. Rhonda, I have respect for your family and especially your grandfather. Sooo, nothing was out in the open for anyone to see."

So we continued to talk and argue. Then we began to laugh. We spent the whole day together and well into the night. Then he said well I have got to go. She will be picking me up soon to head back.

I shocked him by saying I want to meet her, "The one that stole you from me. What does she have that I don't?"

He said, "Nothing," he went on to say, "Rhonda, she's ghetto (meaning wild, street girl)."

"Well, you like it," I said!!!

So, in the meantime, I went to visit across the street with Mr. Franklin's daughter, Jessica and told her what was up. I told her that I was waiting to meet this thang and she said, "I like your style." Jessica and I talked about Roderick and his nasty ways and his good ways. But, she and I both knew that this one was a big one for me to cope with. So, I sat and waited for Shaquana to pull up. Roderick was across the street talking to Joe Joe, a friend in the neighborhood that Roderick grew up with.

Roderick yelled from across the street, "Here she comes, Rhonda."

So I told Jessica to watch this. I approached the car and just then, she got out of the driver's seat and walked around over to the passenger's side. Just as she turned from the backend of the car, I was right in her face.

But as she was walking I heard her mumble to him "Did ya get to see Rhonda?" in nasty sarcastic way.

And just then I said, "Hi, I'm Rhonda," with a big grin.

She said, "Hi," shaking my hand.

I said, "Sooo, how is it living with him?"

She said, "Oh girl, we gotta talk."

And of course, I said, "Oh yeah." But for real, I was thinking the hell with you. Sooo, I pretended to be cool in front of her and Roderick. As he came over, we all chatted for a few minutes. At this point, I didn't know what he had told her about us. But, who cares. And he was careful not to say too much, so I played along with his game. At the same time, I was finally playing with his head and playing mind games. He was sooo confused and couldn't believe how cool I was.

So I wished them a safe trip back and I said, "I will see ya soon." This shocked him and messed with her head, as to the plans he and I had made. Which were really none. But, she didn't know what to think either.

So, I walked back over to Jessica and said, "That was fun." We laughed and gave each other high fives.

Jessica said, "I like ya style girl."

I smiled, walked away and went home.

Now can you imagine how I felt, watching my husband drive off with some girl, going back to their lil love shack in Carrollton? It was hard. But that was what was going on at that time.

While Roderick was on his Carrollton, fling, I had done a lot of thinking about us, and questioning if I even wanted to try and work things out. But this time, I was getting better and it didn't hurt as much. The time apart was actually working for the good.

Sunday morning I got up. The girls and I went to church as usual. Then back to the Monday-Friday work and school schedule.

Tuesday night Roderick called and said that he would be back in town Saturday. If I didn't have plans, he wanted us to see each other. But, I had plans and wasn't sure if I wanted to see him. I told him let's just wait and see. So, the rest of the week passed and I went on about my business.

Early Saturday morning, the phone rang and it was him, of course. He called as soon as he arrived at his mom's house. He wanted to see me. So I gave him and his mom time to talk, because I knew that "mom" would tell me everything that he said. I wanted to see what she thought about us trying to work things out. So I waited for a couple of hours before I went over there. When I arrived, we said hello, hugged each other, excused ourselves from "mom", and went outside in the backyard to talk.

He told me that he wanted to come home. We spent the rest of the day going over our issues, about our arguing, and fighting, and that he has put a damper on things. That it would take time for us to work things out.

"Sooo, when will you get your things and come home?"

He said, "Tonight."

I said, "When?"

He said, "Since I drove here, you just follow me in your car and I will go in and get my things. Then we will leave together."

So, I said, "OK."

We told "mom" of our plans.

We left, just before dark. And the ride there, I felt like I was getting revenge and I was claiming my husband back. Now slut, the next time you run off with a man, do your homework. Find out if he's married and what is really going on.

It only takes about forty-five minutes or so to get to Carrollton from Louisville, so we were there in no time flat. We pulled up to the "love shack" and he went on in. As he made the first trip out to the car, I popped the trunk button so he could put his things in the trunk.

Then he said, “She's not here.”

So I said, “Oh.” And I was thinking to myself, so he's going to grab his clothes and run while she's away, just like he did to me. Hmmm, with a sigh!!!

And then a car pulled up. It was two white guys looking for Shaquana. Roderick walked over to their car and talked to them.

Roderick came to my car and said, “That's one of the reasons that I don’t want her. Cause she's trash. Those guys came over the other night and Shaquana had too much to drink. And she was dancing all nasty and in front of my face. I don't want no girl like that. She’s trash.”

And I thought to myself, he's got the nerve to want someone to treat him right. All that he's done with me and now with her! I didn’t really have harsh feelings directly against her. It's just that he was my husband. Now it was merely a competition thing.

So the guys left. Roderick went back in to get his other things. He came to the door and said, “You can come in if you want.”

So I did. I wanted to see what he left our home for. How they lived in the "love shack".

When I went in, I couldn’t believe my eyes. It was old and ran down. I wouldn’t come here to stay on a weekend fishing trip, let alone live here. Yuck! I didn’t want to touch anything. It wasn’t dirty from them being lazy; it was just dusty. Everything was outdated and just old. You could see where she tried to put a woman’s touch. But, it needed a makeover badly. The house police would have arrested them both. So, I felt good knowing that they weren’t living tooo great!!!

Just then, the door swung open and it was her. She started yelling at him.

“What are you doing? Where are you going?”

Sound familiar? (Smile)

Then he told her that she could stay here and be trash. Those guys were here looking for her again; and she had his permission to go and be with them.

She started crying and ranting and raving, and pacing the floor like a leopard wanting his prey. She begged me to leave so that they could talk.

I said, “No, because they were arguing so. I didn’t want anyone to get hurt, and then I would be a witness to any of this bull. So, I thought it was best for me to stay and see what was going on.”

And then they went off into another room and I heard her say, "I know that I wasn't the best housekeeper. And I know that I didn't spend as much time with you as I could have."

When he came back into the room where I was, he had a smile on his face, and she sounded like me. The way I used to plead to him when we would breakup. And just for a moment, I saw myself.

Then he must have said something really hurtful, because she grabbed a huge knife and threatened to kill him. And he just laughed. And he went outside.

She was crying so that she started talking to me and telling me how they met. And that when he had my car, that she begged him to take my car back, and she wanted me to talk to him and convince him to stay. Because she thought, we were getting a divorce.

I asked her if she was in love with him.

She said, "Uh no. Uh yes. I'm gonna be honest with you. Yes, I love him."

I knew that she had been bit by the Rody bug and that she was on her way down a long, winding road that would lead her nowhere.

Then he said, "Rhonda, ya ready? Yaw don't need to be talking. The hell with her Rhonda! Let's go."

So we left. As we were pulling off, she yelled out the door, "I hope he can get it up. He can't keep it up long enough. So, good luck."

He laughed and said, "The reason I couldn't get it up is because I was not attracted to you. And you were not what I thought you were."

And I thought, nooo the reason you couldn't get it up was because you are married and under God's laws. It wouldn't happen because you were wrong and you had a guilty conscience.

So, we continued to drive and there was silence for the first ten minutes or so. I wasn't gonna say a word because I had begun to feel sorry for Shaquana. I knew that she was devastated and I have been there before. She actually hugged me before I left. I feel her pain and it don't feel good. He's a dog. And why would I help him? That's ok. I won this round.

When we get back home, I'm gonna shock him. I'm gonna let him get settled in and then I could put his ass out. I wanted revenge. He's sooo stupid that he should get his own place and women won't keep putting him out. At this point, I hated him. And he made me sick!!!

When we arrived home, we had a couple of drinks and talked. I had a surprise for him. He was back on the couch again and it would be long time before we'd be intimate again. And just like a little puppy, he went to his couch. We said our good nights and went to bed. He knew that he would be in the doghouse for a long time after this one. And he was humble. I think he was glad to be home.

But me, my feelings had changed. I had won the lil competition of getting him back. Sooo, the hell with him now! He was going to do things on my terms this time and my terms only. Now, who's playing mind games? I'm gonna play him like a fiddle. It was my turn! Now, let the games begin!

I swore from that day on, I'll never go to Carrollton again!

"YOU GOTTA PAY THE HOUSE"

Roderick had just hooked up with a guy that he knew from back in the day. He was excited. I remember thinking to myself, Oh Lord, please let it be someone who would be a good influence on him; someone who didn't do crack or any other drugs for that matter.

So I asked Roderick where, exactly, did he know this guy from.

Roderick said, "Luther Luckett."

Oh hell- the penitentiary. I thought to myself. Roderick was always excited about stupid stuff. The things that "normal people" would get excited about, he would ignore. But crazy stuff like partying or going on a spur of a moment trip would get him going.

He went on and on about this guy. Bradley this, and Bradley that. When I was in the pen, he took care of me. We had each other's back. I found it ironic that of all places for Bradley to move to was around the corner from a jail mate. Uh- one of those things that make you go hmmm!

"Oh yeah Baby, his old lady wants to meet you. Maybe you and her can go walking together."

I said, "Walking? I'm not going to be held up every evening by someone who ain't ready to go walking. And you know that I take my walking serious."

Ever since I knew that I was going to have surgery, I began to plan to lose some weight for health reasons, as well as vanity. Even though vanity is not of the Lord and God doesn't want us to get caught up in the way we look. But when a person loses weight, they start to feel better about themselves and they tend to shine more. Which builds up their self-esteem and then it's on (a new creature).

So I just brushed off the conversation as if it was nothing. I went on walking as scheduled everyday at 6:00 P.M. My walking also helped me to clear my mind as to what day I had. Whether it was the stress from work, the girls, Roderick, or whatever, it was time for Rhonda and Rhonda only. Now anyone could join me, but I was "getting mine" and no one was going to stop me from my exercise.

My co-workers had started noticing my weight loss. I had already lost say about thirty pounds. I had begun to start feeling physically fit, and it helped out with my smoking and my snoring at night. I was feeling better after my surgery and getting my strength back little by little not quite 100% yet, but it was soon to be.

Roderick could sense my confidence coming back. A few times when we would have words, he said nasty things to me like, "You fat ass." But I knew better because I was in a zone and he couldn't change my focus. I was focused, bound and determined. I had a great support system at work. There is always someone on a diet or going to the gym. Sooo, I was in good company and we would encourage each other. I was drinking my water, eating the right foods and really doing a great job. When he'd call me names, I would think to myself, one man's junk is another man's treasure. So I knew that it would be just a matter of time before he'd start getting jealous. He would be losing some of the control he had of my mind.

I knew that someday I'd be rid of him and I would meet someone who really loved me for me and not what I could provide or do. So I had begun to get a new attitude. I would sing in my head the song by Patty Labelle, "I Got a New Attitude". I would also pray to God for strength and patience with my weight loss process. But I know that with God, anything is possible. So I just held my head up. I could hear my grandmother's voice in my mind saying, "Rhonda, you can do it!" At night when I laid my head down to rest, I felt good about me. And that's all that mattered.

The next day just before I struck out for my daily walk, I over heard Roderick talking to someone on the porch. I saw people out there, but I keep getting ready to go. Just then, he opened the door.

"Hey Babe, here is Bradley's old lady. She came to meet you."

I was immediately ticked off because I just knew this was another form of his sabotage of my doing something for myself. Ya know they'll probably want to have a drink and we will be up well into the night. But I went to the door with determination on my face and the strength of the Lord in my heart. He wasn't going to stop me. I hated to look so mean because I would just be meeting these people for the first time and I don't want to be rude.

So I pushed the door open and said, "Hello I'm Rhonda. It's nice to meet you. I'm sorry; I'm on my way out to go walking. Maybe we can talk some other time. You all are welcome to come over one weekend. Maybe we can cookout."

I felt my body moving off the porch. It felt like slow motion.

Roderick then says, "Oh, she's going with you!"

Then I felt the pit of my stomach start to rumble. I thought to myself, damn, now I've I got to be nice. I just wanna go walking in peace.

So I turned, smiled, and said, “Oh, OK. You’re more than welcome. What’s your name again?”

She said, "Toshia.”

I pretended to be sooo happy that she'd be joining me. But I wanted to spit on Roderick and tell him where to go. So, she and I got into my car and rode off. One mind said not to talk at all, just pretend that she's not even in the car. But the other mind said, go ahead and talk to her.

So I started small talk and she could tell that it was not a good time for me. Because I told her, my husband was trying to get rid of me, in hopes that I'd be gone long enough so he could talk on the phone to some girl while I was gone. She just looked at me as if I was crazy. So we talked and exchanged bits and pieces about our relationships and what we wanted out of life and our relationships. I told her that I loved Roderick but I was ready to leave him due to his being back on drugs. She shared with me her man was using drugs too and that his preference was crack also. As we walked around the track, I thought to myself great, my new friend Toshia and I have mates who are on crack. And that we had that in common, how sick was that? I was sooo deep into this nonsense, that even I was stupid. I may as well have been on it also, because I was stupid as hell.

Toshia talked stupid to me, ya know illiterate. But it's not her fault. Sometimes we are a product of our environment. And who knows what the girl has been through. Surely nothing like myself over the past three years! So I continued to talk to her. We had a great walk after all. But I knew that it wouldn't last- her and I walking, because she had already told me that her leg was hurting. She has trouble with her legs at times. I thought, good Lord, forgive me. But, I don't need this. I want to be at peace when I walk and not having to stop and wait on someone. I needed to stay focused and continue my journey back to a healthy state. I was 5'2' and weight about 230lbs and that was way too much for me and my frame. So it was very important that I keep up the good work.

So when we got back to the house, the two men sitting like they were kings or like the "cat that swallowed the canary". As soon as Roderick spoke, I knew that he had been hitting the crack pipe while I was gone. So ya see it was another ploy to him getting rid of me so he can do what he wants. I know this sounds stupid, but I allowed Roderick to do drugs in the house because I was scared for him out on the streets. I wanted to protect him. Besides, I knew that he if got locked up, I couldn't afford to get him out of jail. I also knew that when he got high he wanted sex. I was afraid that he'd get with some "hoochie momma” or a “hood rat" and maybe give me AIDS. So, I tried to keep him close to home.

So we all sat on the porch for a while then we ante'd-up (everybody pitches in) for some beer. We drank for a few hours. After they left, I told him not to have strangers in our home and not to have anyone here doing drugs. He was lucky that I would allow him such. He apologized and then we went to bed. While laying in bed, I told him that I didn't like Bradley and his old lady.

He yelled at me and said, "You always think you are better than other people."

But I knew better because I go out of my way to befriend people. But I had a feeling that this couple was not to be a part of our lives. Since Bradley did crack, we were just asking for trouble. After he yelled at me, I turned my back and cried.

He knew that I was upset and his only comforting words were, "Rhonda, follow me. You need to loosen up and stop judging people."

Well, me being a Christian, or trying to live right, I started to feel guilty. One of the biggest concerns for a Christian is to not offend anyone or hurt anyone's feelings. So I went on to sleep feeling as though I had not only been rude, but I was judging and that I would be judged. I didn't want that because I knew the Lord was not pleased with what was going on in my house anyways. So I asked God to forgive me for all my sins. I closed my eyes.

The next day was the same routine, my walking and us arguing about something- one thing or another. I was feeling myself slowly not wanting to be with him, but I went on as if everything was OK.

As the weeks went on I'd come in from work and he and Bradley would be in our house, our bedroom, no less. And I hated it because I feel the bedroom is sacred and private. But we only had one TV in the front of the house and it was in our room.

So just to keep down on the arguing, I would calmly say, "Honey, I don't want anyone in our room. I may have something out personal. That's embarrassing. So please, sit in the living room or out on the porch."

He'd say, "Oh, OK."

So we then started hanging out over to their house for a change. At first I didn't mind but not long afterwards I was uncomfortable there as well. I started noticing that their house was a revolving door. At first I was intrigued because I wanted to see why Roderick always wanted to go over Bradley's. So I started seeing that men and women were coming. I was very uncomfortable and I felt dirty because I didn't know these people and they just didn't look right to me.

At first, the nights were all of us playing cards and drinking. Then they started to smoke crack. At first, I was ready to go. Then this girl came in. She was about 6'2", very tall for a girl. She was high already, but she came with crack and she was ready to share it. So I sat back in my chair and gave Roderick a look that could kill. He motioned me to follow him outside for some fresh air. I followed him.

When I got outside I said, "What is going on?"

He said, "Oh well, when you do crack, we try to share with each other because when one don't have it someone else does. That's how you learn who you can trust to share with."

I was walking around in circles in the courtyard of their apartments.

I said, "Ya know this crack thing is going too far. And you are beginning to disgust me. This whole scene is crazy! Do you realize that we all could get busted by the police?

He laughed and said, "You are sooo paranoid."

I said, "Whatever. I'm going to stay for a while longer. But in twenty minutes, I'm leaving. I do have a job and children and need to go and handle my business at home."

He agreed. But he said, "Rhonda, I want you to be observant as to how crack affects different people. It will trip you out."

I said really nasty, "No, you are tripping me out." I murmured under my breath, "Going back in stupid dog."

It was about ten o'clock and it was getting late. I went back in to have another beer. As I sat there and watched, I was just amazed.

I said, "Man, this has got them gone."

Toshia and I were the only ones in the room that didn't do drugs. I thought to myself, if we get busted, my defense will be for the cops to test me for drugs and that I was there to pick up my husband. Damn can you believe this? I'm sitting here planning my defense in jail. How messed up is that?!? I have allowed this fool to reduce me to nothing.

So I watched them divide the crack and share each other's pipes. I started getting sick to my stomach. They even would pass the liquor bottle and drink after each other. I thought to myself when we kiss, I'm sharing all these germs with these crack heads. Oh my God! And I put my head in the palm of my hands and said, "Lord, if you let me out of here without getting arrested, I will not come back." So I sat and watched them for a few more minutes. My mind and spirit wanted me to leave, but my body wouldn't move. I was too busy watching how the crack would only take seconds for them to change into another person-right before your eyes. There was about eight of us there at the time.

I noticed Toshia and Bradley over in the corner having words. So I got nervous and I was ready to go before a fight would break out.

Then all of a sudden, Toshia said, "Excuse me everybody. I'm not a rude person. And whatever ya do is your business. But ya gotta pay the house or you all will have to leave." But in the same breath, she said, "Not you, Rhonda. I'm talking about these crack head suckers."

So I looked at Roderick as if I could die. Then they all busted out laughing and apologized for being rude. They all pulled out $5.00 each and placed it in the middle of the table.

Toshia walked over, picked up the money, put it in her pocket. She said, "Thank you. Now I can pay my phone bill."

Then I knew I had to go. This girl is as crazy as they are.

So I started get up to go and I motioned to Roderick and said, "Honey ya ready to go? I need to get ready for work and to check on the girls.

He said, "Ah Baby, hold up. Wait five more minutes."

One of the guys said, "Man, you better go on with your wife."

Another said, "Yeah, she's tired and ready to go."

He said, "I'll be home a little later. By the time you get your shower and get settled, I'll be on home."

But the other men kept trying to get him to go. Well he wasn't budging because he wanted to continue to get high and his eyes was on the tall 6'2' girl. So I knew that he was going to stay. So I said my goodbyes as if it was OK. But as I headed to the car, I realized that he didn't have any respect for me. He didn't even walk me to the car.

Toshia said, "Hold up Rhonda." And she closed the door behind her, followed me, and said, "I wish we could have met under different circumstances."

I said, "Me too." But she knew then I'd never be back.

She said if Roderick ever tries to pull anything at your house with a lot of guys hanging out smoking tell 'em to "pay the house".

I laughed and got in the car. Now, I only lived around the corner. So, I felt safe. As I pulled up in front of my house, I sat in the car and cried. It was awful to see how crack takes over people's minds and how they are so into it. My heart went out to them all. I couldn't believe what my eyes had witnessed. I put the key to the door, and showered and went to bed.

Still no Roderick! I thought, well, maybe he will run off with the 6'2" girl and leave me alone. Around three o'clock I heard his key in the door. He came in took a shower and came to bed, as if nothing had happened. My mouth and throat filled up with spit. I had to swallow to keep from throwing up. I was sick to my stomach and I didn't want him to touch me and to kiss me. Hell no, he's nasty in more ways than I knew.

For the next week, I had little or nothing to say to him. We were not intimate during that time. And the feeling came back to me again, that I needed to leave him and go on with my life. He knew that my feelings were changing also. So we just tolerated each other.

A month or so passed by. I knew that Roderick was still going over to Bradley's house- but the hell with him. I 'm just waiting for him to get his back pay disability check and for him to pay a few bills, maybe get my car fixed and he's out of here. So I went on pretending that things were OK. However, that was sooo far from the truth.

One day I had come in from work, and he was not home. So I was glad and went walking, showered, had a cold beer, climbed up in my bed and began to write in my journal- nothing specific just jotting things down. I had begun to lose my memory. I was so depressed and so out of it mentally. I could hardly remember what we had for supper the night before, my drinking was heavier and my mind was at a loss. I felt that if I wrote down what I was going through it would jog my memories and would stimulate my brain. And I would someday write a book about my experiences with Roderick and I could look back someday and be free of all this madness. I had to always laugh to keep from crying.

Just when I had put my journal down and lay down, I heard the keys turning in the lock. So I pretended to be asleep. Roderick came in and he was whispering. But I heard voices of guys and I continued to pretend to be asleep. Just then, here he comes towards the bedroom. My stomach flinched and tightened in knots and I could feel myself having to use the bathroom. But I lay there quietly. He had the nerve to lean down and kiss me.

I pretended to just be awaking and said, "Oh. Hi, Honey. What's up?"

He whispered and said, "I got Bradley and a few fellows in the living room. We're gonna have a few drinks, then they will be leaving."

So I made no comment, so he'd know that I did not approve. He went into the living room and closed the wood sliding doors together-

and had the nerve to be gentle, as if he didn't want to disturb me. Well guess what too late. It was already about 11:30 and I have to work in the morning. I jumped up and ran to the bathroom. Oh great I have diarrhea. My stomach hurt sooo badly. It was nothing but my nerves. I guess I could feel something wasn't right about tonight. So I lay back down to try and calm myself and try to doze off to sleep. I did for a whole twenty minutes. Lord in heaven, please help me! I tried to sleep but their voices would carry. I turned up my TV and they turned up the stereo. I tossed and turned and tossed and turned, and cried and cried until about 4:00 A.M. - my alarm goes off at 5:00 for work and so the girls can go to school.

Then Roderick came into the bedroom and said, "I'm getting ready to leave, but I'll be right back."

And before I could get up, curse, or yell, he was gone. So I reached over and set the alarm for 5:30. I need every minute I could get. Of course, I still couldn't sleep. I was too angry, but somehow I managed to get about an hour and ten minutes rest. BEEEP! BEEEP! BEEP, my alarm goes off and it's time for work.

Roderick had not come right back like he said, and I went into the living room and looked around like a stranger. I felt as though my home had been invaded by aliens. Everything was dirty and it all needed to be sanitized. They left beer cans, traces of marijuana, crack residue, and cigarette ashes all over the tables.

I cried, showered for work, and started getting dressed. The girls were unaware of anything, but I knew that I had to let them know that Roderick was out partying and would probably be in later. They could care less and that's understandable. They only tolerated him because of me- the love that I had, or the love that I did have. I usually leave the house around 6:30 A.M., take the girls to the bus stop, and head to work. I'm due at work at 7:30.

Just as we were about to cut off all the lights, check to see if the curling irons were off and to feed Gigi, here comes Roderick. I had nothing to say at first. As he was coming through the door, there followed him the other two guys. And this time they brought a girl. The tramp had the nerve to say hi to me.

I said, "Roderick, GET IN HERE!!!" and he followed like some stray dog looking like some fool. I asked, "WHAT ARE YOU DOING?"

He said, "We didn't have anywhere to go, so I brought them here."

Oh, I can't even tell you how I felt. I went into the kitchen and told the girls to go out the backdoor and I would explain to them later. So as usual, the Roderick strikes again with some BULL! So they went to get into the car, so I went back into the living room and told them that I was on my way to work and they had to leave my house.

Then one of the guys said, "Mam, he promised us that we could come back here. We gave him crack all night. And he said you would be cool with it."

I looked at him and he looked sooo stupid- like a jackass. So, I told them, they had 30 minutes and I would be back after I took my kids to the bus stop. And if they were still here, I would call the police.

I couldn't call in sick. I had already been on probation for missing too many days and I only had a few sick days left. So I had to go.

But before I left, I told them to, "PAY THE HOUSE!"

So they reached in their pockets and gave me $40.00 and I took it on my way out the door. I smacked Roderick and called him a nasty dog, and left the house. Roderick knew I wouldn't be back. He knew I was in trouble with my job. So he new he was safe for at least 6 or 7 hours. Maybe I'd be able to leave early, but a whole day, no. And he knew it.

When I got in the car, I was laughing so I wouldn't upset the girls. I pretended that, all was good; I wished them a good day at school and waited for their bus to come. I waved goodbye and drove off as they got onto the bus.

As I was driving, I was in such a glare of tears; I couldn't see the road or any cars. The only thing that snapped me out of it was a car blowing its horn at me. Then I realized that I was at a stop sign, not a streetlight. So what was I stopped for? Oh Lord, please help me. Help me to help myself. I cried all the way to work.

Then as usual, I pretended that all was good. I had gotten so good at pretending that I had fooled myself into thinking that it will all somehow work out. How stupid was that? I knew that they or someone was going to in have sex in my house. I sat at my desk and just kept calling home cussing Roderick out trying to detain him or distract him. But my bosses kept coming pass my desk. So I had to be cool. I didn't need to lose my job on top of everything else that was going on.

At one time, my supervisor said that if we ever wanted to share anything with her, she would be willing to talk and try to help us out if possible. But I couldn't tell her. I couldn't even tell my best friend and co-worker Rosa' Lee. I was in too deep and no one but God would know and understand what I had gotten myself into. I just wanted to scream. Lord, help me! Lord, help me at work. I couldn't eat. I couldn't work. All I did was run back and forth to the bathroom all day.

Luckily, when I got home, the girls hadn't arrived yet and Roderick was sitting in the recliner chair exhausted, I guess. I had such a rough day, that I didn't feel like fighting. I knew that was the next thing. So I just went around the house looking for signs of something not right. I could feel it. Something was wrong.

So I inspected the girls' rooms one by one and Danielle's room looked OK. Then I went into Chanielle's room and stood around looking to see if anything had been disturbed. Chanielle is such a neat child that it would be obvious if anything had been touched. Then all of a sudden, my eyes focused on the comforter. I couldn't believe my eyes. My heart started pounding. My stomach turned. My palms were sweating. I began to pace the floor over and over back and forth. What I had realized is that someone had been in my child's bed having sex.

I SCREAMED, "NO! NO!! NO!!!"

There was hair all over the bed- long weave, and I knew. Then I ran into the bedroom, hit Roderick in his face, and knocked off his glasses. He got up and it was on. We were cursing and yelling at each other.

I was crying, "How could you do this to me?"

He said, "The hell with you. Ain't nobody been in your daughter's bed. All you care about is your kids. Stay here with them I'm out of here."

I said, "Good."

He grabbed me and choked me. I could not breathe. I just knew I would die. Today! Right now. Then he let go and I ran back into Chanielle's room and started collecting the hair. I needed proof to show that he had someone here. As nasty as he was, he probably had sex in here. I want a divorce, and get out. So he came in to the hallway and slammed Chanielle's door. Then I realized that he locked me in the bedroom. And with all my might, I snatched the door, the lock broke and I got out. Then we started fighting all over again. We fought for at least an hour.

Then something stopped me, and sat down and told him he needed to leave. He did, for a few hours. Then when he came back, he asked could he stay until he found somewhere to live, and that we'd get the divorce. I told him he was to sleep on the couch and not even think of ever touching me again. So he spent months on the couch. He came and went as he pleased and I came and went as I pleased.

The reason that I didn't push the issue is that I realized that I was just as bad as him. Taking the money for the house, that basically it was me giving them permission to do whatever they pleased. So I was just as at much fault. At least that was my thinking. For what little thinking I was capable of doing during those days. I barely even knew my name!!! Ya see my whole thinking was off. I had about as much rationalization for things as he did. I had begun to lose my mind. And the only solace I had was I was still smart enough to realize that I was losing my mind.

I know for a fact that I was losing my hair. I know that stress has to release itself somehow. I remember sitting down watching TV and playing with my hair. All of a sudden, I felt an area that was bald. It was the size of a tennis ball. My hair was coming out from stress. I was so scared that I wouldn't live to see my fortieth birthday. I figured I just wasn't gonna make it.

EVERYBODY'S GOT GAME

In this day and age, everyone is looking for what someone can give them or do for them. Gone are the days when two people are drawn to each other and just want to enjoy getting to know the other person. Gone are the days that men respect women and want to get to know their mind, before the behind. Gone are the days when a couple has the desire and ambition to work together and each one brings something to the table.

Nowadays, it's all about what you can get from your mate, and the competition of who's doing the most for each other. Everyone is keeping score, and everyone is sooo afraid of being hurt or used. No one is really trying to enjoy life and each other. Of the two, one is trying to outwit the other, or even manipulate the other. No one wants to just seize the moment, and enjoy life, the simpler things: going for long walks, holding hands in the park, going for long drives in the country or the old fashion family get-togethers.

What is going on! Men play mind games with the women. Women use sex to trap the man. Whatever happened to men taking a woman to dinner and a movie? Whatever happened to women not giving it up on the first night? Doesn't anyone have morals and values anymore? No one respects marriage or the constitution that it stands for. Whatever happened to fathers really being a part of their children's lives, and knowing what was on their minds? What happened to everyone sitting down for supper together? What has happened, to this world?

Nowadays a man expects a woman to wear a size six dress, have a doctorate degree, be able to make homemade family recipes and still have time for a wild night of passion after she bathes and put the kids to bed. She must not only be in a good mood, she must look sexy and pretty too!!! A woman nowadays expects a man to make six figures, own his own business, own a hummer truck, have a Cadillac escalade as the family car, and to place diamonds at her feet. We expect too much from each other and we require too much. What about true love? What about true passion?

There are sooo many different types of relationships these days. There are your traditional relationships. There are the traditional long distance relationships. The traditional marriage affairs, and then the new age ones, like for example, men who date women for years only to tell her years later that he has found someone else and that he is now going to marry. Oh and what about the man, who treats his girlfriend like a queen, has the utmost respect for her and she is seeing another man on the side that only wants kinky sex from her? Or the woman who finally meets the man of her dreams to only find out that he's not only married, but he's gay. And what about the teens that are being date raped or exposed to young guys that have domestic violence tendencies that he has learned from his dad or his big brother! What is going on in the crazy world? What about the minister of a large church that is secretly having sex with one of the church members? Or, what about the doctor that uses crack cocaine and goes to the seedy neighborhoods for prostitutes, to get a way from his suburbia neighborhood.

Looks like everybody's got game.

Friends

How could you hurt me so?
I never wanted you to go.
When you hit me, it was so unreal.
The look in your eyes could surely kill.
I just wanted to be in love and to sing.
I didn't even need a ring.
I wanted to be your wife
And enjoy the rest of my life.
You were my best friend,
Up until the end.
If I had a chance to do it all over again,
I'd just wish that we could be friends.

WHOOPED

Whew, I'm sooo tired! I thought to myself as I sat down waiting to talk to a counselor. I had finally mustard up enough courage to call the Center for Women and Families. I needed help and this time, I knew that I could not do it on my own. I knew that this time, it had to be different. I must prove a point to myself, as well as society, family members, co-workers and everyone that knew me, and my current situation. I had been down this road sooo many times that I literally needed to be helped. When I placed the phone call, I was told to come on in; if I was ready to begin healing and the start of a new life. This was like winning in the Kentucky Lottery; this was a chance of a lifetime. And I knew that I must take this opportunity, or I would die.

While I sat I thought to myself, that at this point nothing matters. I don't care what my family thinks, not even the embarrassment that may come from even walking through these doors. I don't even care what my two teenage daughters might think- God bless their hearts. This is all about me. For the first time in my life, I didn't seek the approval of others. This was my monster that I created. And words from my own dad's mouth, “You can either feed the monster, or you can kill it.”

Over the past three years, I have been juggling many things. I have been trying to hold a relationship and marriage together, raising my two teenage daughters and taking care of our family pet- a poodle named, Gigi. Also, I was dealing with the job related issues- such as being put on probation and not being eligible for the yearly raise or bonus. I have had constant car trouble-including blowouts on the expressway here and there. My having to deal with the complications of having chronic anemia includes missing days at work and being rushed to the hospital from work. I had to deal with the planning and recovery of an emergency needed hysterectomy.

Then there are the child support issues. One father not paying child support at all "like for say fifteen years out of the seventeen years that my oldest daughter has been on this planet earth. And my other daughter’s father wanting to reverse his child support payments back to himself simply because I asked of him for the first time in her life to allow her to come and stay with him and his wife and their daughters for a while. This was so that I could work on my new marriage and all the complications that come with blending a family. My daughters hated my husband for all that he has done to me, as well as them. I didn't think that I was asking too much from my daughter’s father. But he felt like if she would be living and eating at his house then he shouldn't have to pay child support. But, it was just for a while. I couldn't believe that he would be so cynical and sooo cheap. The added stress I felt dealing with his wife and their two daughters making comments on the fact that I had put my husband over my daughter. And that I wasn't spending enough time with her. How dare they judge me! Nothing changed. My daughter and I still continued to walk our two miles a day around the park in our neighborhood- "Flagee Park". And I would pick her up and we would go to church. So why were they so concerned as to how I do things in my life?

On top of this, learning that my husband, whom I thought was recovering from the use of Crack Cocaine was now using again. And all the problems and complications that come with being addicted to drugs: car theft, stealing, lying, manipulation, infidelity, abandonment, plotting, and brainwashing. I had a mother-in-law that would have loved for us to work things out. She worked as hard as I did trying to get Roderick on the right track. I felt really bad for always including her, but I needed her help and guidance. My social drinking turned into a daily routine to help deal with all the stresses that I have been under. And my cigarette smoking, turned from one pack a day- to two packs a day.

While all of this was going on, I was still trying to teach my daughters how to be ladies. And I was also taking them to church and not just sending them like some parent's do. I actually attended the service with them and fellowshipped with the other parishioners. I was supporting them at school functions, activities, and the "Marching Band". Both of my daughters are band students; and have been music students for years. So I have tried to be supportive as much as time allows. Also our time bonding so the girls will feel comfortable and free to share their problems and concerns with me. All the while, I was trying to educate them on sex, peer pressure, dating, drugs, finances, and just life in general. So you see, I needed help!

This morning when I woke up I knew that I would not be going to church. I could feel the depression settling in my bones and moving over me like a shadow. The weight of depression felt as though as someone had draped my body with two heavy quilts. All I could do is cry and feel sooo sorry for being a disappointment to my children, but most of all to God. Someone had to help me, and soon!

I mean like yesterday, I also felt like I was coming unglued at the seams. I was lifeless. I had nothing else to give to my children or my husband. I was out of gas. I had no hope, no desire. If I were to die, it would be better for all involved- suicide? No. I don't believe in it, but natural death? I was ready. I tried everything I knew to make all this work, and to no avail. I felt all alone. Hmmm, the first time I didn't feel God and his angels. But, it was obvious. That God's grace has kept me. I also was grieving the death of my mother and grandmother. I knew deep inside that if either one was still alive; I would have more support. I would not be so alone. I'm feeling that this is all my fault and that's what I get for trying to be nice. I couldn't help but to think, about my family and friends. Where is everyone? Why will no one help me? I felt sooo stupid and irresponsible. Who gave me the responsibility of being a parent anyways- and teenagers no less? Life is crazy and so is the world we live in.

I continued waiting to speak to a counselor, and it gave me a chance to reflect on just the past year alone. It began to make me cry. Thoughts were running through my mind like a movie, bad memories after bad memories. I was exhausted. I needed to shower and to sleep. I thought that if I could take my brain out and put it on the table; I could just rest my brain. That's how much of a break I needed.

"Hello, Mrs. Davis. My name is Kelly. I understand that you have been going through a lot. How may I help you?"

Just the mere fact that someone wanted to help me for a change was a bit much for me to take. So, of course, I started to cry. And then, I began to hyperventilate. She helped me and then coached me through calming myself down. She was very patient and understanding. I was then able to compose myself.

I started out with the last big fall out that my husband and I had. It was during the Fathers Day weekend. But that wasn't the worst one. The Fathers Day fight was just the straw that broke the camel's back. Just thinking back hurts me so, as if it was just yesterday.

"Ya see, Mrs. Kelly, I loved my husband dearly. I loved him from the bottom of my soul- however deep that is, so much love. I had from the first day I met him. I knew that I wanted him to be in my life. I fell for him, and I fell quickly. He was to me, the kind of guy that was considered to be from the "wrong" side of the tracks. He was almost like your biker or gangster, the rough and tough boy type. And I was attracted to him right away. Besides, he was a lot of fun- ya know, the life of the party, the class clown. And he knew anybody and everybody. The few that would slip by he'd pretend to know anyways because the popularity of him being an ex-high school football player, who won all state, and a full scholarship, back in the day (years ago) had went to his head. Now don't get me wrong it was some Dion Sanders type of notoriety, and game winning going on. He really was good and was in the newspapers every Saturday morning for scoring so high and so well in the football game the pervious night. So let's give him his credit. But, all the attention helped in who he'd become a spoiled, self-centered, attention grabbing, womanizer, who at one time had it going on. He had a beautiful wife, two children, home in suburbs, and nice cars- right off the show room floor.

"But twenty years later and after being divorced for nine years, that's when I meet him, down and out, out of the state reformatory (pen) "Luther Luckett" living in his mother's basement. I meet a wounded bird and try to fix it. I met him through my sister. She was dating his brother. I went with my sister one Thanksgiving Day. I was helping my sister take a dish over to her boyfriend's mother's house. And there he was my future husband. The one I'd make mine and live happily ever after. Our relationship started out fun and exciting like everyone else's. And then something happens and people settle in, and the real person comes out.

"I had a lot of reasons to leave him, but I made excuses for his behavior. I noticed that he was changing, but I still married him anyways. I thought to myself, he's just turning fifty years old and he's going through some changes. But I wanted him to be his self, not have to put on any airs, and just be who he really was.

"After one year and a half, we got married against all odds. My children not being too excited about the union and a host of friends and relatives sharing the same feelings; that I was ruining my life. I was in love. I saw signs and pushed them under the rug. Ya have to realize that I absolutely adored my husband. And I had never fallen for a man the way I fell for him. The sex was awesome. I loved the way he smelt. I loved the way his hands felt. I loved the way he'd kiss me. I loved the nights of us staying up talking all night. I loved the long walks in the park. I loved the nights slow dancing by the fireplace. I loved how we'd play in the snow at 3am while the entire neighborhood was asleep. I loved to just watch him work or cook. I was like a bee and he was honey. And ya know what; he wasn't good looking at all. He was short, dark, and had big ears. But to me he was the finest thing going. He had muscles in his thighs from his football physique. I always fantasized of being married to a football player because I was a cheerleader in high school. So, I was in my element. I was in heaven right here on earth. I even had honor in my new married name. It represented honor in our social circle. My husband came from a large family and they were very well known.

"It was about six months into our on and off marriage, that I noticed my husband starting to really change. I had people tell me that maybe he was back using drugs again. But, of course, I didn't believe it because he told me he'd never do it again. Besides, his health was bad. His heart damaged from using drugs years ago and he was recovering from a slight stroke. Sooo he'd never touch the stuff again. But, ya know my husband was also dealing with some disorders. He was bi-polar and he had been diagnosed part schizophrenia. He was on anti-depressants, heart medication and pain pills. And he was being treated for arthritis. So a lot of times, I would blame his behavior on him being over-medicated, coupled with alcohol. And I made excuses for his behavior. I noticed as long as he was high or had something to drink; we got along just fine. But if I wouldn't use bill money for our liquor or for his drug habit, he'd start nick pickin'. He began to never be happy with the house, supper, my daughters, the dog; you name it. I use to watch him come up with issues. So we'd argue and that would give him an excuse to leave and stay out all night. This is when his drugs took over."

"Mrs. Davis, from what you have told me, you are a victim of domestic violence."

"Uh, well I thought that was just in the movies."

"Well let's see, you said that he would put you down- calling you awful names. That he'd refer to you as being fat and out of shape. And he'd tell you that nobody wants you; and that your children were fat and lazy. In an altercation, with Chanielle, he choked her. He threw your dog, Gigi, and broke her hip without any remorse. He'd laugh when asked, "What happened to your dog." And the large hole in the bedroom wall, because he was angry, and was releasing it. Mam, that's called domestic violence. And the fact that you and your daughter were in the home without any running water and your electricity's soon to be cut off is a part of domestic violence as well- not providing for you and your children. You have been mentally, physically, and financially abused, and your dog- that's animal cruelty. He could go to jail for these charges. Have you taken out an EPO on your husband?"

"Ah that's when he can't touch ya right?" I'm gnawing on my nails. Just all this talk brings back so many memories of him hitting me, cursing me out and calling me awful names. And to think that I tried everything, I gave him everything and this is the thanks I get in return: a broken heart, a broken spirit and worse of all a broken marriage? That's what I get for trying to help someone, let alone, fall in love with them? How disgusting is that?

"Mrs. Davis, I think you should think about the EPO. It can be used as a defense if your husband was to try and hurt you."

"What exactly is an EPO? I understand that they are not supposed to come near the wife or the girlfriend."

"It is court-ordered and recorded."

"I just want him to stay far away from me."

The court order will help that come about."

"I'm not too sure about that. I heard on the news the other day, how a guy still approached his ex-wife and still was able to beat and kill her. So she wasn't so protected by the court-ordered EPO."

“Well, just think about it, and let me know if you'd like to. And I will be of assistance to you.”

“Mrs. Kelly, I'd like to learn more about the EPO but I’m afraid to include the cops. My husband may get very angry and start a revenge war, like sabotage to my car, the house, or anyway of hurting me. So I just don't want to rock the boat, or make waves. I just want to be left alone. And I'd like to start a new life.”

“OK, Mrs. Davis, that's fine, I understand. Mrs. Davis, would you like to come with me I'd like to show you around the center and show you, where you will be staying?”

“Ok, Mrs. Kelly, I will have to leave and go pick up my daughter, Danielle. She is at work. She should be getting off work around ten o’clock. OK, that's not a problem. My daughter works at Kentucky Fried Chicken, and has been for about a year. She is doing such a great job.”

As Mrs. Kelly showed me around, she kept referring to the “shelter”. Well that took me back a bit because "shelter" has a negative connotation. And even with me, I thought “Me, staying in a shelter?” Well, just for a second I had to check myself. I'm no better than the next woman that is here. So how dare I put myself above anyone, especially as much as I have gone through?

Well I know that no one should label themselves. We live in a society that will do that. And it will cause us to sabotage ourselves without even realizing it. Through the Christian belief that I have tried to learn, study, and honor, I do believe that death lies in the power of the tongue. This just means to watch the words that you use. We can condemn ourselves or our current situation; just because of what we say. So if we talk negative we start to believe negative because we are giving our brain the message of what we are actually hearing. Then we adopt it and then we are a product of our own doing. Like say, “I’ll never get a job.” Well, with that attitude, you have already set yourself up for failure. So, it's best to stick to the old saying, "If you can’t say anything good, don’t say anything at all.” I truly believe in the old wise sayings because what was good then, is still good now.

So I decided to refer to the shelter, as "the center" it would make me feel better. And that way I will stay in a positive mode and not start to think negative- and will not stifle myself. I walked carefully beside Mrs. Kelly as we toured the center. We first entered the room called the family room. There were about ten ladies sitting in there. Some were watching TV and others were laughing and talking. Some would speak, and others just look at me as if I had just stepped off of a flying saucer. Then, I was shown the kitchen, which was totally disgusting. I tried really hard not to show my disgust on my face. I had to constantly remind myself, that I must at all times, give thanks for having a safe place to stay, so I can get back up on my feet. So again, I smiled and kept going.

Mrs. Kelly explained that each woman had a chore to do and obviously the one assigned to the kitchen had not abided by the rules. Surely, by this time at night, all chores should be completed. The rest of the center was fine. Then Mrs. Kelly showed me our room which is known as the quiet living room. It is a place that the center uses for the woman and children when they just need a place to get away, on occasion it is used for someone when the center is full until space is available in an actual "room"- the space in the center comes available as someone moves out, if they are exited for breaking the center rules or whatever the center deems to be inappropriate behavior such as: drugs, fights, stealing etc.

"Mrs. Davis, this is your room. Now, you can relax and shower. I hope that your night is restful."

With tears in my eyes and I know a grateful expression on my face. She could tell that I truly appreciated her help and the center. Mrs. Kelly was an angel that God had put before me. "Thank you Mrs. Kelly," as I closed the door and sat down on the love seat that was also in the room. Sigh. "Whew! Thank you, Jesus, for giving me and my daughters a roof over our heads. Thank you, God, for the escape from my husband and all the turmoil that I had been going through. Thank you for a safe place."

My thoughts then turned to my daughters. I don't think they would like it here, let alone live here. Sooo, I had to come up with a plan, a schedule- ya know a time frame. So they will have some tangible goal and see in the near future that we will only be here, for "x" amount of time. I think they will receive it better and their spirits will be enlightened. It is very important for me to let them know how important to me this stay is. That I need the center for a place for me to re-group, get back on track and begin to start a new life all over again. A new life that is more stable and healthier, as well as safer.

So I really need to look at the center as a resort type environment. It's all in the mind- how you look at things. My stay here is an all-expense paid vacation, free room and board: three meals a day, free laundry facilities and free cable TV. I could actually save some money and pull up myself up by the bootstraps literally. Also, we will have around the clock classes: self-esteem, domestic violence, relationship and stress management classes, all free, as well as a private therapy session as often as needed. It's a one-stop shop. This place is like "Home Depot" they have just about everything a person could want and any tools you need to get the job done.

Oh, it's almost time to go and pick up Danielle from work. I was sooo excited to share with her all that I had learned about the center and I wanted her to see that this is exactly what I need. I had picked the right place to come for help.

I knew that this was it for me. I actually made a conscious decision all by myself. I have always needed the approval of others, and was always was concerned about what they thought or how I should do this or what they thought about that. Well, not this time. I didn't want any outside influences. I knew this was to be my decision, and mine only.

Every time me and my husband broke up somehow through family members, we'd get back together. So I didn't want to hear their opinions anymore. I was ready to take charge. No more of people making choices for me. I need to be in it and live it. And this was the first day of the rest of my life. So whatcha think about that? That's my new way of thinking, and I'm happy!

I was pumped (excited)! I didn't even tell my family for the first two to three days because I didn't want to take the chance that my husband would get wind of it. So I kept this a secret until I felt secure and then I made it known that this time, I was really leaving my husband. After the repeated breakups over, and over, and over my family would have just assumed that it was just another breakup and give us a week or two and we'd be back together again as usual. So this time, I showed them who was in control, me-and here is what I plan to do this time.

Oh, it's past the time to pick up Danielle. I'd better go. Whew! The drive from the center to my daughter's work is just about fifteen minutes drive, not too bad. But from our home, it's about five minutes. So it will take some getting use too.

"Hello Mamacita."

“Hey girl.”

That's what my girls call me from time to time. We love to speak Spanish, just not fluent with it.

“Oh Mom, how's the place? Are there kids there and do we have our own room, and is it nice?”

“Well hold up, slow down. I'll tell you, OK? This is the deal. The place is fine except the kitchen. Well I’ll just let you see. And also, this is a lesson to you all about the times that I've told you that keeping your room clean was important. You'll get first hand experience to see how it will effect your first impression."

I explained to her the rules and I told her to put her things in the room. I gave her the grand tour, and I looked for facial expressions to see if she was OK with things. It was so far sooo good; until we entered the "KITCHEN". She just said," Uh," as we left the room.

When we got back to the room, I said, "OK, what do you think?"

She said, "How long do we have to stay here? I'm not eating out of that kitchen!"

And thought to myself, gotcha!! It worked. Now she sees the importance of keeping a clean house. And what a lesson to learn and especially, when she's preparing to go to college. Of course, I'm the mom so all that I say is crazy right now, because moms know nothing. Yeah right! I guess I've lived for forty years for nothing. Oh well, time will tell and one day just, like I did with my own mother, she will appreciate all the teachings that I have tried to pass on to her. She will come to me, one day with such pride and honor, that she had a mother that truly loved her and wanted nothing but the best for her in spite of all my shortcomings that she witnessed while growing up.

"Danielle, we need to wash our clothes and get ready for bed."

So we spent the rest of the night getting unpacked and washing clothes because we hadn't had water at the house to wash and our clothes had started to pile up.

We began to talk, about the plans that I have made and the goals we have to meet. I explained that we would set our goal to be back at home at the end of August. Which now it was June twenty-second, so two months at the most. Our goal would be, to be back in the house, the week before school would start which would be August 18, so give or take a week or two.

So in saying that you could see the stress lifting from her face, and she smiled and said, "Oh that's nothing we can do that."

So I agreed, and we gave each other a high five and a big hug. I said, "The good thing is that you work and now that school is out, you will be working some mornings and you will be coming and going. Oh and band camp starts in three days. So, that will keep you busy too."

And she said, "You're right."

So then we picked where we would sleep. She choose the love seat and I said, "Of course not, you can have the bed."

And she said, "No mom."

Then I said," I insist. For all that I have put you through; you deserve a good night's rest. I will sleep on the love seat."

Well, I tried to get comfortable. And then I said, "I tell ya what, give me one of those mattresses on your bed." It actually had two.

And I threw it on the floor and she cracked up laughing saying, "No you didn't, Mom. You're not sleeping on the floor."

And I said, "Oh yes I am." And we both laughed and I cut the light out and let out a great sigh of relief, just knowing that my daughter and I were safe. We both had a shower, and some place to have a good night's rest.

Just as I began to say my prayers, she said, "Mom?"

"Yes?"

"I love you."

"Yes baby, I love you too!"

"Good night."

"Good night, see ya in the morning," a big smile went over my face. Then I said," Thank you God. Thank you for everything, and please watch over us like you always do. And thank you for blessing me that Chanielle is with her father and maybe the two of them will bond and become better friends. Amen.

I slept like a baby. I woke up feeling revived. And on my way to work, I kissed Danielle on her forehead and told her that I loved her, and to call me at work when she's about to leave to go to work. I wished her a good day and left.

When I arrived in the parking garage, I said a prayer for my safe arriving and for the Lord to continue to watch over us like He always does and then I got out of the car. As I walked to the building, I began to get paranoid, almost as if I had a sign on my forehead stating that I live in a shelter, and everyone could see it. The sign also showed that I was a failure and that I had allowed myself to be dragged down by a pack of wolves, and that I was sooo stupid. But all of a sudden, I could hear myself say, hold your head up and don't look down. You have survived and you should honor yourself right now at this moment. So with honor comes glory. So I sighed and smiled and said," Hallelujah," and went on in to work.

My workday was going as usual, and it was a typical Monday, with the regular Monday happenings such as: the copy machine needing paper before I could use it and my password not working so I had to call the security number to be reset for a password. So things were back to business until one of my co-workers asked me how was I doing and I said just fine. Well I knew it was a lie, but this was my business and they don't need to know.

Now at work in my immediate department, there are four black women, and we have round table discussions on a daily basis. We talk about our weekends, our children, our cars, and our pets- no holds bar, but this I was keeping to myself. Besides, just like my husband would say, and repeatedly put in my head, that no one really cares what you're going through anyways. I thought he's right, it's not like any of them would open their home to me and the girls anyways. They don't need to know. They will surely just talk about me behind my back, so what's the use?

So I continued to sit at my desk. Finally keeping a secret- the one thing that my husband said I couldn't do. He always said, "Rhonda, all you do is tell people your business. People don't care. You're stupid for putting your business in the street." But I always knew that he wanted our life private cause if anyone knew that I allowed him to do drugs, cheat on me, and most of all- hit me. They'd influence me by saying, to leave him. See, his mission was to isolate me from anyone who would see what was really going on. So, I pretended that everything was fine, even when they were extremely bad, because I loved him sooo. And he would straighten out soon and get use to the girls and being married again. So I believed him and continued to live a lie. So there, Roderick, I'm finally keeping a secret and you're not around to see it. I smiled and continued to work.

After work, I had to remind myself to go home a different direction. I had a new home and for me not to make a turn in the normal direction- ya know we become creatures of habit. And most of us will take the same route home and to groceries. So just out of habit I didn't want to go towards my old home. That's funny and besides, lately I forget things too. So I sorta talked my way, walking out of work to get on the elevator.

When I arrived at the center, it felt sorta weird and a bit uncomfortable. But just upon entering the building, I saw Mrs. Kelly's face and she asked how my day was. Wow, she really cared! So I stopped and talked a bit and left with a smile on my face and headed upstairs on the elevator to the floor where I stayed.

Ah, the quiet living room was waiting on me and I just needed to be by myself for a few minutes to regroup before heading into the family room. After about thirty minutes or so, I went to the ladies room, freshened up my make up.

After a deep sigh, I thought to myself, I need to go meet the others that I will be living with and try to make some new friends. I was scared, but I was ready, come what may. Last night, some were not too nice- it appeared, so here I go! I held my head up and spoke to anyone that was in my sight. Whether they'd speak back or not was their deal. When all of a sudden stood before me an older black lady: short and somewhat stocky, with a beautiful smile.

She said, “Hi. Would you like for me to show you where the soft drinks are?”

And I said, “Yes, please.” And we began to talk. She showed me everything: how the stove worked, because it was a big commercial stove- the restaurant type; told me where to find all the can goods and anything else and told me if I needed anything to just holler. Her name is Mrs. Robinson. She had made a point to make me feel comfortable and actually feel at home.

So after fixing me something to eat, she and I sat down together and had supper. She continued to give me the ins and outs of the place. She told me about the cliques and about the ones she had deemed to be nice and easygoing. I told her that I smoked cigarettes and she even went down to the smoking area with me to show me where it was, so we talked even more. I felt comfortable with her and began to tell my story as to why I came to the center to stay, and she shared hers. She too was abused and it was sooo sad because she was the grandmother type and who would lay a hand on her? But she went on to tell me that she used to be on crack cocaine and I couldn’t believe my ears. And that it lead to some of her abuse episodes. My heart ached for her. I just wanted to kiss her and we both began to cry, reassuring each other that things would be better for both of us. And it would be soon because God don’t like ugly and He will bless us for being strong enough to get out of the situations and living conditions that we were in. So we knew our blessings were right around the corner. She also shared with me that she had just been diagnosed with MS- Muscular Sclerosis, a bone crippling disease, and she was struggling with her speech already.

My heart was so heavy. “How can I help her?” I thought under my breath. Oh my God, if there is anything I could do or say, please give me the words to encourage her. And all of sudden the words just flowed right out, as if I was a professional counselor or something. And then we bonded. From that day on, we were friends. I noticed as the days went by she had great respect for me, like I was "God".

I felt so special and honored, and felt that God was truly using me, and working through me, because there are a lot of people hurting. I'd be an extension of Him in letting the world know that He cares, He knows their troubles and by His grace, they will be all right. Ya see in this crazy world that we live in; people have to endure sooo much that it's easy to feel alone; to feel that no one cares. But God constantly reminds us through others that He does care and that we will never be alone. That if we just have faith and support each other, we can get through anything with Him by our side. But in rough times, it's all hard to believe.

As the days went on Danielle and I began to make lots of friends and we began to open up and relax. But something I noticed was happening. People began to look forward to seeing us. It was sorta weird, but at the same time, it was inviting.

One night, I asked Danielle if she felt the same thing I was feeling. She agreed.

She said, "Me too, I've noticed it. It's like we're rich or something, ya know- like royalty. They look up to us and always want our advice."

And I said me too, and we just laughed.

And then I thought for a while and I said, "That's it!"

And she said, "What Momma? Whatcha talking about?"

"We have added a good feeling to the atmosphere. We make people laugh, and they can feel the love that you and I share for one another. The Lord is using us here, and they can feel it."

And she said, "Yeah, you're right. I think so too,"

I realized that for some of the people here we are the only hope they have and we give them a chance to see how life can really be when it is filled with love. Even though we have problems too, we can still be happy and smile. We haven't just given up or we're not sitting around being depressed. We're pressing on. And it's all with the attitude, as to how you handle things. See you and I both know that the Lord watches how you go through problems and how you handle yourself when up against the wall. He will test us. The Bible says that if I can trust you with a few things I will make you ruler over many. So yeah, we're rich, "rich in love." And yes, we are a part of royalty; we're God's children. So now, whatcha think about that?

And we both prepared for bed and slept till the next morning closing our eyes knowing that the Lord has a purpose and that everything happens for a reason. The Lord will put the right people in your life at the right time for the right reason.

I have always been a person with a big smile. Over the years I have been complimented on my smile and how pretty and white my teeth were, and just being a bubbly happy person- ya know "pure sunshine" that's me. Well one day, I was going down the hallway at the center and there were two ladies having a loud confrontation about something over what a child of one lady's said, about the other lady's child. So it was starting to get out of hand. All of a sudden, Mrs. Kelly walks up and as I was passing by, Mrs. Kelly said to me, "Rhonda, have you met Doris and Angel yet?" I said "No, not formally." So I said, hello and they both mumbled hi, but it was not a warm greeting. And all they wanted to do was to continue and I was in the way. So I looked at Mrs. Kelly, smiled, and sorta rolled my eyes in amazement that these two were going at it so. I went on to my room thinking to myself as, wow, that's a trip! Whew! Glad that's not me, involved. So I went on to read and prepare for bed.

The next morning it was on to regular business. Each day when I'd come in to the center, I had already mapped out a schedule for me to follow so I would stay on task. So I could meet my goals. Not only does the center have a tremendous support system, they have a group of employees to work with you on your own individual case. Each client, that's how the center referred to us ladies living in the center, had assigned to them a caseworker. They would help you with government issues such as: Social Security problems, address changes, child support, Section 8, disability, and any government concerns. Then, each client would be assigned to an advocate, which is your partner- sorta like your personal assistant. She would see to it, that you had what you needed from clothing for interviews for a job, to extra bed linen, to an extended curfew, to transportation, anything that would aid in helping you to meet your goals. They would go over with you as to what your goals might be, like getting a job, moving into your own apartment, finding daycare so you can work, or just having someone to talk to on a regular basis, so that you can began to heal.

So by me working during the day, when I got in, I would go straight to my advocate or caseworker, to touch base as to what I had accomplished so far and what I needed to do next. So I always had my folder in hand and some of the ladies that didn't know me thought that I worked at the center and would ask me questions. I'd help but I told them, "I'm a client I live here just like you."

And they would say- you do? Well it's the way you carry yourself."

From that point on I became Mrs. Rhonda. I had the respect of the actual workers. Isn't it something? Wow! So on this particular day, I noticed that Doris was crying and I asked if she needed anything or if she wanted to talk. If she wanted to talk let me know. Now Doris is a big lady. She's about 6', large in stature, the look, "don't mess with me," and she also has an attitude most people would be scared to approach her and definitely not have a casual conversation with her.

But I wasn't scared because if I don't like ya, I don't mess with you either. So I will try once, but after that the hell with ya. I didn't have the tolerance for others that I had for my husband. Other people only got a chance or two, unlike my husband. I gave him chance after chance.

Doris began telling me she was having trouble with her daughter not having respect for her. Also that she was jealous of the relationship that I had with Danielle. So I began to explain to her my battles with my girls and what has worked for us. And I even told her that she'll see what I'm talking about when Chanielle comes to visit this weekend. She will see not only the difference in my children, but she will see how Chanielle's mouth and attitude will be. Also, the struggle I have had, trying to raise a daughter that thinks she's a grown woman already.

We began to bond. Doris stressed to me that, "At first I really didn't like you."

"Who? Me?"

"Yes."

"Why?"

"Cause you came in grinning and smiling and all happy and stuff. How in the hell can you be happy living in a shelter?"

So we just laughed and gave each high fives. I told her it's all in the attitude and how you choose to feel. Do you want to have a pity party or do you want to move on and start a new life? The mere fact the center literally saved my life, because I was about to lose my mind. So therefore, I'm not ashamed to be here. It's a blessing. And she could feel me, and she understood.

I think that the ladies feel comfortable talking to me because I keep it real. I do claim being a Christian. I also know that I'm not perfect: I curse, I smoke cigarettes, I watch inappropriate TV, I go to clubs from time to time with my friends; but I'm human. I have been exposed to worldly things too, but nothing stops me from constantly trying to better myself and trying to stay focused. I'm always working on myself and improving areas, trying to live right and treat people right. I'm always conscious of what areas need to be worked on and I set goals and try to reach them. The day that I'm perfect, the Lord will call me home to be with Him. Until then, I will live the best way that I know how. Sometimes I even play the lottery, but the God that I serve doesn't expect me to be perfect. But He expects me to keep working on my faults, and to be real and honest. To me, church is in your heart, how you live and most of all how you treat people. It is very important to be true to yourself, and to enjoy life. Why waste time brooding? Why waste time crying and being depressed? Ya gotta have the attitude of "you need to laugh to keep from crying", and remember that weeping endures for a night, but joy comes in the morning. So that is why I feel that the ladies here relate to me- just keeping it real.

Today is Friday and Chanielle is due to arrive around seven. I'm excited to finally have the three of us back together again. I'm also nervous because I'm not sure how she will feel about the center. So it will be interesting to see her reaction- what she thinks and how she feels. I need to go to the store and get my errands out of the way so that every minute can be spent with my daughters. A mother's job is never done. A mother is always trying to please and wants everyone to be happy.

"Hey Mom," Chanielle says as she walks into the center.

"Hey Baby. How was your day today? "Did you have a good band practice?"

"Uh it was ok."

"Ah ok. Well, I'm sooo excited! Come and let me show you around."

She looked excited as well. First, I introduced her to Mrs. Robinson, then Doris and her children. They all were glad to meet Chanielle and glad to see us back together as a family. Chanielle was at ease. She really didn't say too much about anything. She was just glad to be with Danielle and myself. I was relived to know that she was cool with everything. Chanielle and Danielle started to get involved with the children: playing games, watching movies, doing arts and crafts, and just being kids again. For sooo long they were angry and had a lot of built up frustration in them. It was such a blessing to see them relaxed and having fun. Just for one moment I looked at them being sooo peaceful and my eyes filled with tears, my chest was full and a lump in my throat. I said thank you, Jesus.

I walked over to Mrs. March, looked her in the eyes and said, "Thank you sooo much."

She said," You're welcome."

Mrs. March was the crisis counselor that took my call when I called in the center and I would forever be grateful to her. She was sooo kind to me on the phone. She was the one that told me to pack up my things, come, and take the first step in starting my new life. Mrs. March is about 6'2", a tall black woman. She has the presence of a sergeant and that's what we call her "March the Searge". She doesn't play. When she is on duty, you will follow the rules and that's just it. As far as your chores, you don't leave on a Saturday pass until you are checked off the list showing that you have completed them. Now she's a beautiful person and will do anything to help you, but don't cross her. She's lots of fun, and truly a blessing for the center.

We have been at the center now for about one month. The girls and I have gotten comfortable being here and calling the center, "home". We have learned the public bus routes to work. Some days I would choose to take the bus because it was sooo convenient and I enjoyed letting the bus driver do the driving. Some days I had to catch the bus because of car trouble. Ever since my car was wrecked, it's not been the same.

Once when Roderick and I had split up, I decided to go shopping for a new car. I had been driving a little white hatchback, a Geo Prism and had driven it for years. But I allowed Roderick to drive it while I was at work. He tore it up by driving like someone crazy. He didn't care it wasn't his. So he "dogged it". So I finally chose a Ford Thunderbird. I was sooo excited and was sooo proud of myself. I had the car for about one month when Roderick and I got back together. As usual, I let him use the car while I was at work. He was sooo stupid. He would be late picking me up from work and sometimes he wouldn't pick me up at all. I would get a ride from a co-worker, Nadeen. I was sooo in love that I would always forgive him and let him drive anyways.

So one night we had just got back from an outdoor concert on the waterfront and I had just stepped into the shower. He said, "Hey Babe, I'm gonna run around over to Lamar's house- a friend of ours. I'm not staying long."

So I said, "OK. Hurry back because it is already sooo late and you have been drinking a bit."

He said, "Just about twenty minutes."

I said, "Oh alright."

Well it was about midnight when he left. Around one o'clock he still was not back, so I went to bed and just prayed for his safe return. Our relationship at the time was going well, no arguments and everything was good for a change. I was happy and in a comfortable state of mind. I had seen him at times going out of his way to work on our relationship and be the man that I wanted. So, I had no reason to think that he was up to no good, even with his history of disappointment after disappointment. But I loved him and we'd soon get married, and what was mine was his. After sleeping for a few hours, I woke up to use the bathroom. He still was not home. So now, it was about 4:00 A.M. and I began to worry. All the negative thoughts of the past started flooding my mind, and I started to feel sick to my stomach. I began to beat up on myself saying things like: you're sooo stupid for trusting him, he's a dog and he will never drive my car again. All those earlier thoughts of sharing were gone. Then I prayed, "God, if you let him bring back my car safely, I swear I'll never let him drive the car again."

So I went back to bed and tossed and turned and tossed and turned. I had a terrible headache. Somehow, I dosed off for a few more hours and then I heard the key in the door. I turned my back and pretended to be asleep, just like in the movies. I waited to see what he would do, if he would wake me or just go to bed. He reeked of alcohol. The strong scent filled the room. The smell of stale cigarettes was in the air also, which made me gag as if I was going to throw up. So I continued to lay there. He took off his clothes very slowly and quietly. He eased into the bed he didn't even disturb the covers. He lay on top and I waited till he fell asleep. When I heard him snoring, something told me to go and look out to see if my car was OK. I did. I had to open the door because we lived in an apartment and we had no front windows, just a front door on that side. When I opened the door, my car was not there. So my throat filled up with that lump again and I started crying, went back into the bedroom, and immediately woke him up.

I said, “Roderick, where’s my car?”

He sat straight up. He was out of it, from being so high and drunk. He said, “Uh, uh, I don't know.”

And I screamed, “What do you mean you don’t know?”

“Uh, uh, it ain't out there?”

“Hell naw! Where’s my car?”

“Uh, I got car jacked.”

“What? Did you call the police? Why didn’t you call me?”

“Uh, they robbed me and took what money I had.”

So I had to calm down. I sat on the end of the bed, and I said, “You have to tell me exactly what happened, because I'm gonna call the police and make a report.”

He started with, “Well when I left here, I went to Lamar’s just like I told you.”

“Ya had better be telling me the truth because I’m asking Lamar tomorrow.”

“It's true.”

“And what else.”

“Uh, uh, I parked your car and rode with him and Timothy. They wanted to go and see some guy and I just jumped in with them. So after that they brought me back to the car, about one hour later. Lamar told me to come back over to his house later. Because Lamar was hooking up with this girl and then us guys will hang out more. Sooo, I just rode around and I stopped to call Lamar at a pay phone. While I was sitting in the car, a guy came up to the window and put a gun to my head and told me to get out of the car. He took my wallet and I just walked home. I was scared to call the police."

"Why?"

"Cause I was driving drunk, so I wanted to come home and sleep it off first."

So out of disgust I got up and walked out of the bedroom, sat on the living room couch and just cried and just felt sooo bad and so used. Then I needed to make the call to the police and report what had happened.

It was now Sunday morning. I called and sat waiting to hear if the police had found my car. By the end of Sunday night no information had been reported. So for work Monday, I had no transportation. I called in sick. I wasn't lying. I was sick, sick to my stomach. I had diarrhea from the stress and worry, dealing with him and dealing with the loss of my car. The whole time I was waiting, I kept saying that I was going to prosecute whoever stole it. If they find someone driving it and he just kept saying, "I didn't do it, I was robbed."

Well considering all the lies he had told previously, I had no doubt that he was. I knew he was lying and I played it off as if well, "We will find out who did it." And he kept saying, "Rhonda, if you get your car back, you better just leave it alone. Those boys probably had something to do with drugs. You better just leave it alone." Well "bingo" he's guilty otherwise he would encourage me to prosecute.

So three days later, the police called me and said, "We found your car and two people was in it driving and they have been arrested."

And when Roderick heard the news, he said, "I told ya. I told you I had nothing to do with it."

I was sooo excited to go get my car. When I arrived, my car was wrecked. The entire front was dented in. So I cried and cried. So ya see Roderick has been a problem to me for a long time. So I have been driving a dented-in wrecked car for the last two years, a car that I only had for a month before it got wrecked. Seems to me if anyone should wreck your new car, it should at least be the owner of the car. And now that I'm trying to get back on my feet, I plan on getting a new car by the first part of the new year. So now, I just have to deal with the car and all the problems until then. It's a constant reminder of the ways that I allowed him to dog me and the things in my life.

Today is group. On Tuesdays, we have a rap group session on domestic violence. On Wednesday it's on self-esteem, and Thursday about relationships. So I'm looking forward to it. I love going to group because you can learn sooo much and I especially love group because of the instructor. Her name is Nadira. She is also my advocate. Nadira was such a welcoming to me and my girls upon entering the center. I was assigned to her. Her job was to be a one-on-one support system to me. Nadira is sooo beautiful. She represents to me a strong black woman. She is from East Africa and has an accent that I adore. She is here in the states to continue her education and working here at the center is a part of her educational journey. She also has two teenage daughters and they are beautiful, very educated, and talented young ladies.

One night Nadira asked me and the girls to join her so we could talk about how the domestic violence in our home had an impact on them. She wanted them to have a forum to vent and clear their minds as to how they felt and give them some insight on how things can affect you if your surroundings are negative. We talked for about three hours. I really appreciated her taking out sooo much time with them, and me as well. The girls received it well and gained a different respect for all that I had been through. Nadira felt it was important to explain to the girls how it was like I was trapped in and sucked in like a vacuum. That Roderick took my kindness for a weakness, and how he set out to destroy us, as a family unit. And all the things that I was going through- that I was powerless, because I was in love and my mind was all about him.

See, during the times that I would break up and make up with Roderick- time after time he hurt me again and again- my daughters started losing respect for me. And they started not trusting me because I would disappoint them by being late picking them up, from school activities and late picking Danielle at work because he wasn't ready to leave a party. Or, not taking them places and making them catch the bus because he said that they were too dependent on me. I let him rule almost everything and they had started to lose faith in me.

So Nadira made a point of telling the girls that it was like an addiction. I wanted to make Roderick happy and I would do anything to do so. When you are in love as much as I was, it can be like a drug. Also the facts that I was: brainwashed, manipulated, used and abused. I wanted for them to give me a chance to redeem myself. And the fact that I came here to the center for help was my first step to recovery and the rebuilding of our family bond. The center was like a hospital for wounded hearts and that it takes time for a heart to heal and that for them to patient. And while she explained to them, I cried the whole time. I was sooo ashamed that I had been reduced to such a level. And I was ashamed to be called a mother. Just knowing that this memory will be in my girls head for the rest of their lives was disheartening to me. I knew that I had to win my honor back as a mother. I also apologized to the girls and told them that I take full responsibility for all their pain for the past three years. I asked them for their forgiveness and told them how much I loved them. Nadira played such a role in their acceptance in me and I loved her for that. I knew that this was a tough job for her, but I felt her sincerity and her love that she had for us as family.

So Nadira and I bonded, as if we were blood sisters. And she and I have become great friends. As a matter of fact, I would try to play it off when I'd see her after my getting off of work because I didn't want the other clients to feel any favoritism, but I was sooo happy to see her. She would light up my day. I would actually look forward to seeing her after work. And if we were having her group, I was in heaven. Her groups were very relaxing. We'd start out with candles lit; and we'd do relaxation exercises, and breathing exercises. Then we'd either read poems or go over DV (Domestic Violence) materials. Then we would have a discussion on that topic. Say ah a topic like... manipulation and how it can be used against you in relationship. Also, topics on the signs of abuse, what constitutes abuse, grief and loss.

Most people don't realize that you must mourn a divorce or a relationship breakup like you do a death of a loved one. Just like when you first hear that a loved one has died, the first thought is denial. And so is with a divorce-you don't believe it is happening. Then you start to question why they died and how- and you do the same in divorce. You say, "Why? Why didn't it work?" And then you grieve the holidays. Just like a death, your first Christmas without your loved one is like the first year you have been divorced and alone on holidays without your husband or boyfriend. Then, finally acceptance. You finally accept that your loved one is gone and they won't be back. The same goes with a divorce. When the final papers are signed, it is over!

So in these classes I learned sooo much. That's why I go and it's a very important part of the healing process. Now the center does not make us attend group- it's not mandatory- but it's encouraged. And I tried to encourage others to go and see if they would like it. It would be helpful to them dealing with their journey on the road to recovery.

Nadira and I agreed to visit each other when I leave the center-like go out for drink, to the movies, a play or something. We both wanted and enjoyed our newfound friendship and wanted to keep the lines of communication open. The other clients could see how close we had become. It was obvious. Nadira is cool.

“Hey, tonight the TV is reserved for 8:00. *Waiting to Exhale* is coming on.”

“Yeah!”

A loud murmur went over the room. We have all seen it a hundred times, but it's an excellent movie. We all have TVs in our rooms, but the family room has cable. So, we take turns watching shows. It will be fun tonight because we’re all ready for a good movie and we all want revenge on our perpetrators- the men in our lives that have abused us. What a perfect movie for a bunch of women to sit around and watch.

“I'll make the popcorn.”

“I'll make the cookies.”

That’s how it is here. We all pitch in, cook for each other, and help each other. OK, we all have twenty minutes before the movie.

“All kids in the bed for the ladies that had children under fifteen.” They had to have their children in bed by nine- it was quiet time for the adults. Besides, TV is inappropriate at that hour with some of what’s on TV these days.

Sometimes we have group ourselves. We sit up and talk all night- just like a big slumber party. We work through issues and help each other come up with ideas- you know two heads are better than one, so sorta team work. We ask each other for help like: babysitters for the next day while another goes job-hunting, or if someone needs a ride, we do each others hair, we share reading materials, trade movies, and give each other advice on how we look before a date, what to wear for a job interview, and so on. It's like living with a big family. We have fun with each other’s children. Some of us go shopping together and out to dinner. We just have lots of fun. We laugh together and cry together. I will miss this when I leave from here and go back to the "real world”.

“Whew! She got him back in the end.”

“Yeah, dirty dog.”

Giving each other high fives and just loving watching the movie all over as if for the first time. That was fun. And we all continued to talk and share our experiences with each other.

“Hey ya'll, we sound like a bunch of men haters.”

“Hell, we are!”

“Hahahaha!”

“Hell, yeah!” With a big roar of loud laughter like someone told a joke that had us all in the floor.

Theresa, who is known in the center as a player- ya know "playa playa". Theresa is white girl that only dates black guys and is married to a black man. She enjoys partying and hanging out. She is the life of the center. She keeps us laughing. We sit up late at night waiting to see whom she met today, what he looked like and where did they go. We wanted details- and she'd tell us. Now Theresa comes from the country and talks like she from the hills of Kentucky- with a slang dialect. Imagine that- a country black girl- a sista. Theresa is cool. She always dresses so cute and she is the fashion police. She will lend you an outfit for a date- let you wear anything that will enhance your look. She will help you pick out what you are wearing.

"We ought to line up all the men and shoot 'em."

"Hell naw! Save one of um. I need somebody."

"Damn girl, you're crazy." And we all burst into a loud roar again.

"All ya'll are crazy. Hell, I'm going to bed."

"Yeah, me too."

"And me to." So that was the end to a great night of fun with the girls.

"Please sign in ladies. Today's group is on self-esteem and Mrs. Jones is the instructor for this group." Mrs. Jones is little and petite. She's about 4'11"- little ole lady, but she's funny. She has us laughing all the time. We love her groups also. She was diagnosed with polio as a child and had to wear leg braces growing up. So, she suffered abuse at an early age being teased by the children in her neighborhood and school. So she can relate to us as to our abuse by our "perps". She also walks with a limp and she looks like she off balance. And a lot of times, she says that people think she's drunk. But she had us cracking up when she made the statement that they need to watch her when she's been drinking because she walks straight. "Hahaha!" She is such a caring person.

She was also assigned to me to work with me as a counselor. So Mrs. Jones and I are cool. She told me that the reason that I was sooo acceptant to Roderick's behavior with the abuse is because of my brother's issues. He is an alcoholic and we have tolerated his behavior throughout the years. And that's why it was not a "red flag" to me- choosing a guy who did drugs or drinks. Because it was accepted and it was normal in my life where another woman may have ditched him as soon as she knew he was using drugs and drinking.

A lot of the woman at the center was exposed to abuse as a child and it's normal in their household for a man to hit on the lady or the children. So for the women that think why would we settle for such, doesn't know about what has happened in our lives, that would make an easy target for abuse, or why our self-esteem is so low. But most us have been abused somewhere in our lives; that has broken us down and made us vulnerable. And the men that we choose see and use it. And our poor selection of men comes from our low self-esteem. Our job is to find out where we broke down and made ourselves such an easy target.

I believe that mine comes from when I was at the age of fourteen years old. My mother accused me of having sex with my stepfather. Now I was young and I didn't know that my mother was a heavy drinker and her self-esteem was low. She was very paranoid and always thought that somebody wanted her husband. She even accused her sisters before. I was able to get over the hurt and the pain, and we did fix our friendship before she died. But my self-esteem was ruined at an early age. I wanted someone to love me because I felt my own mother didn't or she would have never accused me. So by the time I started dating, my self-esteem was so low that my choice of a man was low. If any man showed me any attention, I fell for him. Because I thought he loved me, which made me vulnerable for all the rejects in men that other women wouldn't give a second look. I was sooo caring, and I wanted to fix the men that had problems- because I needed to be needed and to be loved. So, all these years later I'm now a victim of abuse because I fell for a man who showed me attention, knew my weakness, took it, and ran with it.

So I think that whatever happens to you in your life that is traumatic will and can affect decisions that we make. And if you don't deal with your issues as they happen, they will rear their ugly heads later in life and continue to cause you pain. So you have to grab your tragedies by the bullhorn and nip it in the bud right then and there. I looked at my husband as a "project". I was going to fix him and make him right for me. I needed to fix him. I wanted to fix him. But he needed to fix his self. It starts from within.

Since my mother accused me, I felt like the black sheep of our family. So, I dated black sheep guys, tried to make them whole and fix them. In the process, I lost myself. You'd think it'd be really simple in a relationship: girl meets boy, girl and boy have things in common, and girl and boy have fun and enjoy each other's company. But during all this, girl never thinks that boy would hurt her or cheat on her. And girl gets heart broken. It begins to affect her self-esteem at an early age- of not being good enough. If she's not strong-minded or has support system, she is doomed. Early on, a girl will settle and compromise what she really believes in. If she's not careful, then it will follow her, the rest of her life- settling just wanting to be loved.

People have told me before that my self-esteem was low or I wouldn't settle. But love should come natural and if you love someone and treat them the way you'd like to be treated then everything should be OK. But it's not that simple. Nowadays so much comes into play. Who has what? What they can do for each other. What a person will give you or provide for you. Whatever happened to just good ole fashion love? Do relationships like that happen anymore? If so, who has one?

Today is the first day that I actually allowed myself to think about Roderick and reminisce. But it felt dirty. Ya know cheap- fake. I had different feelings as to what we were, and what our marriage was about. You know the old saying, "nothing from nothing, leaves nothing." That's it we had nothing. I read a poem today that states, "Stop knocking on a wall hoping that it will turn into a door." Roderick is going to always be a wall. He will never be a door, so I need to realize that and move on.

I guess what started me to think about him is that he called me today at work- acting as if nothing had happened, as if we would just pick up where we left off. Just for a moment, I listened. Even though I know that he doesn't deserve a conversation with me. But, I allowed it. I felt safe because I knew this time was different. While being in the center, the classes and my support system had build up my strength not to be so weak to fall for his sweet-talking. So I heard him out. And after the phone conversation, all he did was to reinforce the fact that he still is a liar. That he still is so disgusting. And the fact that I'm away from him is perfect- just what I needed to get my head together. The space away from each other- see we had a pattern, and it was just like trying to heal a broken leg. Just as soon as it would heal, I'd start walking on it. Just as soon as I would start to heal my heart and try to go on with my life, he'd call and say sweet things and I'd fall back in. But, not this time. Before hanging up, I told him not to call me anymore." I don't want you, don't want to see you." And that I was filing for a divorce, through legal aid.

Due to our situation dealing with domestic violence, they will pay for it. Besides, I don't have the extra two hundred dollars or more, not right now. So that will help me out with that, and I can move on. At first, I wanted to keep my name, because I was dedicated to the marriage even though he wasn't. I felt like I had earned it. That's crazy though. So I decided to get my maiden name back because he had no respect for the constitution for marriage. It obviously was a joke, and it didn't mean anything to him. So why would I want to carry a name that represented nothing but a broken heart, lies, adultery and pain? By me coming to that realization shows me that I'm growing, I'm learning and I'm beginning to heal.

After a woman divorces she must feel like used baggage- at least I did. I know that life goes on, but I shared everything with him. I had no secrets. He was my best friend. In spite of all he did, I still loved him. The thought of him hurting me makes me sick to my stomach.

It's been at least a month now. Our wedding anniversary is next week- July 11, 2003. It will be our first year wedding anniversary, but we have known each other and dated since November of 2000. We dated and lived together on and off for a year and a half before we got married. I need to make plans for that day, since were not together. I don't want to be sad. I need it to be a celebration of me being a survivor of a bad marriage and to celebrate my starting a new life. It's kinda hard to do with your heart on your sleeve.

And whenever I take a chance again with a guy, I'd like to keep my morals and values, and be honest about my past. But what if I open myself up again and this guy sees me as being vulnerable, and thinks that I will allow him the same- that I did Roderick? Will the next man try to hurt me too? Or will he use what I share with him and use it against me, and just automatically think I'm weak still? Or will he truly love me for who I am and not use my past mistakes as an opportunity to take advantage of me? I'm sooo scared to try it again. At the center, they teach us to allow ourselves at least a year, to work through the hurt and pain, and our own personal issues. But right now, a year doesn't seem long enough. I feel like I need ten years before stepping back out there- and then, will it be safe?

I also don't want to fall into the trap of hating men. That's not healthy considering that I'm a woman and I have needs, wants and desires. So what's a woman to do?

Fate, circumstances and making some bad choices had changed my life before meeting Roderick. I had just accepted a new job, with a new company, and my children and I had just got back from a beautiful vacation in Aruba. I was in my element and I was excited about life. I was on a roll and not holding back. I had been on a celibate journey for three years. I was involved with my church, my career and my children. I didn't even talk to a man on the phone. No sex for three years. I needed to find out who Rhonda was and what she was about. So my focus was just on the joys of life, family, friends and my God. I did learn a lot about myself. I thought that I had grown to be the woman the Lord wanted of me. So therefore, I thought for sure now I'm ready for a husband and a stepfather for my children. I was serious about life and I was living it.

When I met Roderick, I felt that he was special already due to the fact that he had such a great relationship with his mother. He would call me at work to tell me that he'd be out of the house for while, because he was helping his mother with her errands, that they was going grocery shopping, to pick greens, or to lunch together. And I thought, "Wow, he's really good to his mother." And the fact that mine was deceased, I loved to see people with theirs and how they would spend time together. It was special to me, and he scored big points. I'm sure it helped in my choosing him to date. I figured that if he loved and did for his mother, he'd love and do for me. I have always heard to watch to see how the man you're interested in treats his mother and the other women in their lives. It would be a good indication as to how he may treat the lady in his life. By me trying to be spiritual, I'm sensitive to people and I look for good. Then I try to allow a person to be themselves and not have too many expectations of them because I would want the same.

Beep. Beep. Beep. Beep- reaching to cut off the alarm off. Today is Friday and I get paid. I'm going shopping after work. It's the first time that I have had extra money. I have not been able to buy myself anything for three years other than a purse or some work shoes. All of my money has gone for taking care of Roderick, the girls and paying all the bills. I have been wearing the same work clothes season after season, but today I need some new summer work clothes. Besides, all that walking me and Chanielle have done over that last four months after my surgery; I look good. I have been a plus size woman since I had my children and never lost the weight, or dieted and lost and gained back and some bonus pounds. But I have always tried to dress nice, but the clothes I wear are outdated.

Being here in the center has allowed me to save a bit here and there. So I deserve it. While I'm at it, I will treat the girls to something nice. They have not been able to shop either. Things really changed when I met Roderick. I started living from paycheck to paycheck and most of the times not having anything.

I remember the day that Roderick called his self showing me some affection. He said to me when I got home from work, "Honey I know you are tired right?"

And I said," Yes."

So he said, "After dinner, I want you to go into the living room and get on the couch with your favorite book. I will play your favorite CD. And I will take all calls and just tell whoever calls that you're sleep."

So I said all right and I began to relax. Just as I nodded off, I thought to myself my purse! I didn't trust him because by now I knew that he was using drugs again. And I felt like the little money that we have I need to keep out of sight. But I thought to myself, "Surely not. He wouldn't be sooo nasty." So I continued to relax. After about an hour, I felt revived and joined him in the bedroom. And I said, “Thank you honey. That was sweet for you to allow me some time to myself.”

And he smiled and said, “You welcome.”

About a half hour later he said, “I'm gonna walk over to the post,”- which is a neighborhood place where the old army retirees hang out.

And I said, “OK. See ya soon.”

I knew that he wouldn’t be gone long because the post closes at ten. So that was ok with me. I thought to check to see what bills are to be paid tomorrow and what errands I need to do. So I checked into my purse and counted my money. I noticed that he had stole money from my purse while I was relaxing in the living room. I then started crying and couldn't believe he would stoop sooo low. How dare him! I do everything for him. I have given him my last few dollars just so he would have some money. I loved him just that much!

Of course I brought it to his attention when he came back home. He apologized. But it ruined the rest of the week for me. The thought of him being sooo selfish really hurt me. It seemed to me his mission in life was to make me miserable and I was too deep into him to turn back now. But I knew deep inside I was being treated like a fool and that I deserved better. But I was in love. I would just pray and beg God to make everything OK, so we could get on with things and just grow old together.

"Hey Rhonda. Whatcha doing tomorrow?” Theresa said standing in the door of my room.

“Ah I'm not sure. But, it's my wedding anniversary and I don’t want to be in here, ya know. I took off work tomorrow because I don’t want to be at work crying and grieving my ended marriage- all of ten months. And you really can't say ten months total, because I told you what happened the day after we got married.

“Girl check this out, we got married on Thursday, July 11, 2002. We got married down by Joes Crab Shack on the waterfront. That morning when I left the house, he seemed to be OK. I kissed him on his forehead on my way out the door, as usual and said, ‘I will see you this evening.’ Now Roderick’s job was just to get us the rings and I would pay for and handle everything else, because he wasn’t working. He had filed for disability and was waiting for it to come through. But it didn’t matter to me. I was marrying him because I loved him- including all of his faults. And money wasn’t an issue, even if I had to work a second job. It would all work out. And with love, you can conquer all!

“I was sitting at my desk and the phone rang and it was Roderick. He sounded sad and I ask what was wrong. He said, ‘I wasn’t able to get our rings.’ And I just put my head in my hands and took a deep sigh. I told him, ‘Honey, don't worry. Rings have never kept a marriage together. We can get rings anytime, maybe for our first anniversary. I just want you and to be with you for the rest of my life.’ Now that was to make him feel better. I was use to him disappointing me. So, this time was no different. But once we get married, it will be different. I will be in charge of our finances, so we will be OK. He's just immature for his age- and a lot of men don’t have it together. So he just needs me to help and we will be just fine. So we hung up the phone.

“My heart was racing all day- I was excited and scared. But I just contributed it to what is called,” cold feet". It will all be ok. So I anticipated leaving early all day and couldn’t wait for two o’clock to come. I was getting married and I was marrying my best friend. That's what you’re supposed to do- marry your best friend. I'm such a sentimental person and a romantic that I chose an object to be a sign if he and I were to be together. Throughout our dating, I use to point out ‘Hey, there is a butterfly.’ And I chose a butterfly as my symbol of a sign. Roderick thought that I was crazy and he'd laugh at me. But, he would just smile and say, ‘Girl, you are crazy.’ But no one could tell me in my mind that the butterfly was not a sign. We use to laugh sooo hard because I'd say, ‘Hey Honey, there’s a butterfly. How cool is that?’ And he'd say, ‘Real cool Rhonda. We’re in a park. That's where butterflies will be, ya think?’ Hahaha! So I would go on believing in my butterflies. So over the years, we had joke after joke after joke about these butterflies. We even told our family members and they'd laugh and smile with us. So it was interesting.

“Ya see my mother and father tell of a story when I was a child and I use to ride my tricycle. And there would be these butterflies out while the children would play. Well there was this one butterfly that would always seek me out of all the children and would hang around me by riding on the back of my tricycle. So that's one reason I chose the butterflies as a symbol. I just assumed that me, and butterflies are connected somehow. And another reason I chose a butterfly is that during the years of my celibacy a girlfriend and I said that we would ask God to show us a sign if a man was the one for us. My girlfriend Lynette chose a "rainbow" and I said, ‘Oh you hardly see them. Why didn’t you choose something that we see on a better odds basis? A rainbow only happens every now and then.’ She stuck to her choice and I said, ‘I'm sticking to the butterflies.’ Besides, butterflies are beautiful elegant and free. So that's what I sticking too.

“So after all this time, my associating butterflies with our relationship; it seemed as if I saw butterflies, in unexpected places.

When no others were around, one would just fly pass us. While walking, they have just appeared out of no where- and even out of season, we have spotted butterflies. It began to even trip him out. I said, 'I told you the butterflies mean that we are meant to be.'

My heart was pounding; my palms were sweating. It was almost time to get off work- to go and marry my best friend. I decided to go downstairs to take a break and have a cigarette. And just think and relax before the big event. While I was standing out front of the building that I work in, there were many people walking by as usual. It was noisy from the sounds of the cars and trucks on the street. Then all of a sudden, I realized that I was alone. So I took a deep breath and then out of nowhere came this huge butterfly. The biggest one I had ever seen in my life. The first thing I did was started smiling- knowing that it was a sign and I was about to marry my best friend. So it was all good! So in total amazement, I let my eyes follow the butterfly- just to see where it land. And lo and behold, he came to the trash can- not even a foot away. And he sat there and flapped his wings. So I thought it was my mother, my granny or God giving me a sign. And I began to get really nervous at the same time. I then noticed the color- it was black. And my heart fell to the ground. I felt like I was making a big mistake, that I should wait and not get married. But how can this be? This is supposed to be a sign that we are to be together. But, why now? And why a black butterfly? So, my eyes filled with tears and my heart with sadness. I was sooo confused. Then all of a sudden, the butterfly opened its wings wide open. And it was the most beautiful blue that I had seen in my life. So I began to smile again and just said to myself, 'Rhonda, you're silly. You are too old for signs; just follow your heart.' So I knew then to go and be with my best friend and marry my husband.

"I couldn't drive home fast enough. I only live fifteen minutes from where I work, but it seemed as if I drove for an hour. When I pulled up to the house, I was sooo nervous. But I took a deep breath, put the key into the door, and turned the key. I started feeling really nervous. All I wanted to do was see his face. It would tell me if we would be making a mistake or not. And he said, 'Hey, what's up?' I said, 'Oh, nothing.' I was trying to be cool and play it off as if I was OK with everything. So I said it's time for us to go or we will be late. He said, 'Oh OK.' But I could tell that he was piddling around. He picked up some jeans on the bed from where he had been doing the laundry and refolded them. I could tell he was nervous but I didn't think anything of it. I said, 'Come on, Honey.' And he said, 'You and Danielle go ahead and I will be out to the car.' So we walked on out, and he followed. But he seemed to be OK. Just a bit nervous; but so was I.

"Now looking back, I realize all that was going on. He knew then that he really didn't want to be married. And that he had opened his mouth and now it was too late to turn back. He claims that he did want to get married. But I couldn't tell. He never treated me like a wife."

Yawn! Today is suppose to be a beautiful day- weather wise, the news said, "Sunshine all day." That's good. Well, today is my wedding anniversary- but no husband. What's a bride to do? Oh well, I will make this date- July, 11,2003 a day of celebration: of my being free from bondage, free to live again, free to date some man that really appreciates me for who I am and someone to treat me like a real woman.

So let's have fun today. "Girls, let's go shopping, and have dinner at a nice restaurant and let's just make a full day of it."

"Yeah let's do it!!!"

As the day went on, I would try not to think of Roderick at all. So every thought of him that came to mind, I hurried to erase and think of something else. I would just think of anything to alter my thoughts. At first, it was hard and then later it became easier and easier, so I knew then I would be OK for the day. I decided to get a manicure, a pedicure, and to buy myself something nice. The day was going well. The girls were so happy and it made me think of old times- the fun me and the girls use to have before Roderick came into our lives. It was a grand day. It was beautiful and it was nice. It felt sooo nice to be making my own decisions for myself.

When I refer to being brained washed, it's because Roderick would constantly feed me comments such as "Rhonda, you are not following me. I need you to follow my decisions when it comes to bills and stuff. You are always trying to be in control." Which was reverse psychology, because then I would begin to feel guilty thinking that I was not allowing him to be in the man role. So I would let him say as to how much to pay this or that. And of course, it was never the entire bill. Which then the next month we would owe more money. And he'd never have anything to contribute. Out of the three years of us being together on and off, I'd say in total he has paid about $3,000 compared to my $10,000 or more because I paid for everything. He would always hustle to make money, conveniently enough, for his beer, cigarettes and crack money. He wouldn't even buy his self clothes. He'd just wear clothes that he has had for over the years. Mostly outdated and it was obvious. Like the Olympic sweatshirt that had all the colors of the Jamaican flag and it was held in the year 1988- or something like that. And this is the 2000's. So ya see what I mean. And he would wear "Michael Jordan sneakers that was so outdated the logo had changed. None of the new Jordan's has the word "JORDAN" spelled out big. But you couldn't tell him anything. He thought he was it. Yeah he was full of it.

I can remember the way that he would try to cause division in our home with the girls. Such as, he would have already talked to them before I'd get home from work. And talked about what plans they may have for the weekend. Then later that night, he would tell me.

"Boy! They got your whole weekend planned."

And I say what do you mean?

Well they want you to take them shopping; and they want you to take them to the movies. "Damn!" he'd say, "and I wanted us to go to a party."

He always tried to point out things that could be a potential problem. Then he would say make 'em catch the bus. You ain't no taxi cab driver. They are teenagers. Let them catch the bus! He was always a step ahead of everyone. That's only because he had all day to think of things while we were at work and school. And he loved to cause trouble. He was a forty-seven year old tattletale. He'd tell on the girls like a kid- always reporting and always complaining, just sitting back looking for an opportunity to start some confusion.

What amazes me is that no one who knew me could understand why I was allowing such pain in my life. And why don't I just snap out of it. People just don't realize that I had never been with a man that was sooo good sexually. It's not like I'm a virgin- because ya know that's not true. But I had never experienced the true freedom to express myself. That is until Roderick started requesting sexual acts that were not appealing to me. He would try and convince me that a threesome was normal and that I should allow such. He also wanted to watch me have sex with a woman in his presence. The thought of either request was disgusting. I thought he loved me. Why would he want to share me with someone? I would only entertain his suggestions- just to change the subject. But in the back of my mind, my heart and soul would ache due to his request. The mere fact that he knew that I would do anything to please him, wasn't enough. He wanted to strip me of my dignity and my self-respect. He wouldn't be happy until he had totally ruined me: mentally, physically, emotionally, and financially. He wanted nothing left of me. Nothing, not a shred, or anything that represented that Rhonda was here. He wanted to destroy me.

And the control he had over my mind and my heart was the reason that he could even get into my head. Normally, I'm such a strong person- bound and determined. But with him, I was powerless. It was a spell of such, almost impossible to explain, Sooo much sooo that it scared me. Not only could he light up my day; he could in fact destroy my nights. And he knew the control he had. I was like a robot- a Roderick pleasing robot. And that's all that mattered. I was to please him. In the end of our final breakup, he was very nasty. He talked to me as if I was nothing. He had no concern as to how he made me feel. It was all about him, and no one but him. I was obsessed in pleasing him, keeping him, wanting him to love me, wanting to save our marriage, and I just wanted everything to fall in place.

God showed me many outs. God showed me many of his faults and gave me warning after warning. God even spoke words to me, "Don't look back." After a major breakup we had after him leaving me, Roderick had a pattern of abandonment. He'd just pack his things while I was at work and be gone when I got home. He had done that at least three times: one week after us being married, once after I took him back and thought everything was OK and he moved to Carrolton once. Roderick would flirt with girls right in front of my face and contribute it to his friendly personality. Roderick's nickname is Rody.

So I say, "Watch out world! Rody's loose! There's a guy out there that will destroy your life. Watch Out! He's out to get women who are weak and lonely."

Today in the center we have a church visiting us. We're celebrating Christmas in July. Well I have always heard the expression on TV commercials, but never seen it put into action. We will be going downstairs to the conference room and everyone is excited as to what it will consist of. The mood here is great. The children are excited. We wait with anticipation! Wow, as we walk in the room is decorated beautifully; there is soft music playing and a room full of smiling guests from a local church. "Come on in. Merry Christmas!" Gifts were everywhere. And there were games set up for all to participate in. The atmosphere was very nice and welcoming. Lot's of refreshments: cookies, cake, brownies, juice, milk, and lots more. It was fantastic. As I sat and observed the room, I thought to myself. This is fantastic. These people took out time to think of us- living in a center and dealing with the issues that we have to deal with. This was a welcomed break to take our minds off of our problems and just to be able to relax and enjoy one another. I felt sooo blessed to be a part of this day. As I sat there, I began to thank God. All the children were allowed to receive gifts according to their ages. And each child received, I'd say at least five gifts each. And it was like Christmas. The gifts ranged from porcelain dolls to Harry Potter books, stuffed animals, building blocks, trucks, and Barbies. It was perfect. We couldn't thank the church enough. We took pictures of the fun and celebrations and thanked them for such a great time. It was beautiful. God was constantly showing us that people do care what you're going through and that they will help whenever they can.

Damn, I want a beer. I haven't had one since coming into the center and I use to drink every night to relax. So I think I will go and get a beer. And go to the house and drink one. Ya know, just to get a way from the center a bit and just relax in my own home and space. I know that I'm not an alcoholic cause I've gone without for a month. But I do crave an ice-cold beer. I wonder what that means. Nothing I hope.

The center life was beginning to get a bit uncomfortable because everyone's real goal is to be back in their own home or to get a new place of their own. No one really wants to live communal life. I'm grateful to have a roof over my head, but I want to go home. I miss my privacy and I miss my things- ya know. I miss my collection of horses. Sometimes I would just sit and enjoy them. I have horse statues in all types of materials: porcelain, copper, leather, glass, and horse memorabilia. I love horses because they represent strength and they are beautiful. And I love art. I love the lines and their body structure. I can't imagine their little legs holding up the rest of the body. It's unreal! Oh, and their speed! That's exciting too. How fast they go. And I miss my dog- my poodle. Since being here in the center, the humane society and the center have been working together; keeping my dog, while I heal and prepare to go home.

Mrs. Elaine has been taking care of Gigi and has been there by her side while she had surgery due to Roderick throwing her into the wall. She was injured with a broken hip. The surgery would have cost around $500. They donated the money; due to Gigi being a part of domestic violence. What a blessing. I don't know what I would do without my dog. She has unconditional love for me and always wants to be in presence. She even loves the way my clothes smell. She always snuggles on a T-shirt or a jacket that smells of my perfume. And she wants to be with me everywhere I go.

DIFFERENT CULTURES

SAME PAIN, SAME STRUGGLE

Domestic violence spares no race and no economical background. At the center, I was able to meet woman and children from all around the world. There was an African woman from South Africa named Abeni and her son Camba. A woman from Kosovo named Fikra and daughters Vitore and Shpresa. A woman from Israel named Anissa and her daughters, Reyna and Gavriella and son, Ilan. A young mother from Russia named Tatiana and her newborn son, Sacha. Also, a woman from Mexico named Materia and her son, Javier. I met black and white woman as well.

Communication was difficult at times. Can you imagine trying to tell your story in another language knowing that the chances of being heard and understood are slim to none? Being afraid, not to mention, not having someone you can talk to daily, like the other woman could.

I tried to communicate with the foreigners as much as possible. It was hard. They could hardly understand the basics such as, "How are you today?", "Can I help you?", and "You have a message." We all take things for granted. I know that had I experienced problems with domestic violence and had no one to talk to it would have made things worse.

Some jesters we all have in common might be, a wave or a nod and a smile. So we just all went around smiling at each other. Being a victim of domestic violence has many faces. I always thought it was a Lifetime movie, but never realized I would be a part of it. The clients that were of a different language had additional problems like learning the bus routes, job hunting issues, the meals, and customs. My heart went out to them.

It was an overall confirmation that domestic violence is worldwide. It doesn't matter where you come from. Domestic violence is all about control and manipulation- trying to be the "ruler" and the "King" Women submerged in verbally and emotionally abusive partners suffer deep wounds because we could just look in each others eyes and we could feel each others pain. Our injuries are not visible to the eye. We go through our private agony in silence. We often downplay our misery and pain as if it is nothing.

I often wondered what their story was, but ya know it doesn't matter because pain is pain. The children are sooo adorable. However, they have the pain also. I was so grateful to be here in my country and have never had such an appreciation for the states.

HEALING

My healing started to take shape almost seconds, as I stepped in the door at the center. As I began to feel free, I was the lost sheep that the Lord sent the shepherd out to find.

My aunt sings that song beautifully in our church choir. She always touches my heart while singing it. I often thought of that song on my journey. The song mentions that there was a shepherd looking after his sheep there on a mountaintop. But there were only ninety-nine. He couldn't and wouldn't rest until he found that one lost sheep.

That was me. And the Lord and his angels wouldn't rest until I had been found. And here in the center, I was rescued and I have been saved. Over the weeks and the months, I began some self-healing.

It's amazing what God will put on your heart or right before your eyes. So one day at work, I was reading my emails and I came across a section of inspirational readings. One of the sections was Poems. It read,

"And the day came, when the risk it took to remain tight inside was more painful than the risk it took to blossom."

Which meant to me, that is was more painful for me to stay in the marriage, than the risk it would take to blossom and grow. And it hit me like a ton of bricks. It worked for me. I knew that I had to make a change in my life and current situation. So that was the fire I needed, along with many other encouraging words and wisdom from others. A co-worker knew my pain, because she too had suffered from domestic violence in her marriage. She was very supportive.

One day I came in to work and she had, left me a card saying that, "God never meant for us to go through the tough times alone." That was sooo special to me. I will never for get that day, and the spirit in which she gave it to me.

All of the group meetings I attended helped also to give me strength daily I needed it to make it from day to day. The smiles from my dear friends and co-workers helped to push me along. And there were the co-workers that would treat me to lunch knowing that I had no money. For months, I had no more than five dollars in my purse at a time. I was broke and I mean broke. It was sooo hard for me to stay focused and pretend that all was well.

As I began to get strength, I wanted to pass it on. So I would pray and ask God what I could do to make a difference. And out of nowhere came the idea, to fix a booklet that would in fact encourage other clients upon entering the center, words of encouragement and tools to help them to stay focused and on task while they take their journey to recovery and healing.

I shared my booklet with Nadira. She shared it with departmental heads. The next thing I knew, they wanted to incorporate it into the centers "welcome booklet". I was just amazed how the Lord was using me as a tool of inspiration to others. What a revelation, and a compliment from the heavens above!!!

So ya see; everything happens for a reason. I was at the center for more reasons than the obvious. I went in for help, and ended up helping others. How cool is that? God is good!!!

One day, I was doing some writing on forgiveness and decided to write a prayer to God in reference to my husband. This is what I prayed.

"Father in heaven; hear my cry. Father, I have once again disappointed you. As I bow down before you, I ask for your forgiveness and ask that you continue to bless and watch over me. Father, you showed me many times that this was not for me. But, I was selfish and I wanted to marry my husband anyway. Father you also showed me over and over ways to get out. But, I was stubborn and I wanted to do things my way. So you stepped back and allowed me the desires of my heart. Father, I put him before my own children, before my family and most of all before you Father. I ask that you please have patience with me and allow me to redeem myself.

"Father, I ask that you watch over my husband and protect him. And Father, please let him know that drugs is of the devil and that he could have such a better life if he'd follow you. Father, please speak to him and help heal him. Father, please let him know in his heart that I truly loved him and that I would do anything to help him. Please let him realize that I must go on with my life and that I will always have a special place for him in my heart.

"All these things I ask in the name of your darling son, Jesus Christ. Amen."

I shared this prayer with Nadira and she asked if she could read it during group for the other clients to see how important forgiveness is to healing. I said yes and she announced during group that I had written a prayer. So she began to read it. And one by one everyone started to cry. They felt my pain, my sincerity. And not a single person in that center had a question as to how much I loved my husband and how badly I wished our marriage would have worked. Even Nadira couldn't finish reading and had to excuse herself. One of the other clients finished it. Everyone was crying; even the clients that didn't believe in a higher power. But they felt the spirit that night in our group. After group was over, the majority of the clients came and thanked me, and kissed and hugged me. I know that the ones that were on the borderline with their beliefs were no longer. They knew that there was a God.

From that night on, some of our late nights were about the Bible and God and His mercy that He had graced us with. I also looked at the other clients as brothers and sisters in God's eyes. I had bonded with many of them on a personal level. They had confided in me things that they had not even shared with the staff. They would ask me to pray for them at night and I would ask that they pray for me, and my daughters.

I began to work on a personal letter that I could leave with them when I left to go back home. I wanted them to have the same encouragement as if I was still there with them. I was not boasting; it's just that Lord allowed me this glory and with glory comes honor. I wanted to honor my brothers and sisters with a goodbye letter and it read like this.

"Thank you for making my daughters and I feel welcome. Thank you for listening to me, and allowing me to be free to share my problems with you. Thank you for being there for me when I needed a shoulder to cry on. And thanks for all the fun, the movies, the late night talks, and the dinners, and all the nights in the donations closet. And I hope and pray that we will keep in touch, but if not, I will continue to pray for your recovery and your meeting all your goals. And ya know me 'God bless you'".

And it was a hit they all came and thanked me. Some even cried. I had once again showed them that the Lord is here and He really cares about the brokenhearted and the broken spirits. But He will always show you through someone else that He cares; and that he also knows the pain of sorrow.

I felt that my work was done. I had followed out what God had asked of me.

LISTEN...

By Tonya Jordan

Listen to the sounds of peace
Listen to my heart as it beats
Listen to me breathe
Isn't it great…
For I'm at such a powerful state
Listen to my soul, as it stands tall
Nothing wavering ooh no
Nothing at all
And listen to my spirit make a call...
Upon, the depths of it all.

SHOOT OUT AT HIGH NOON

I had gotten back in bed after taking the girls to their bus stop. This would be my first day at home and I wanted to relax and enjoy being back in my house. So I had breakfast and laid down to rest. I was not taking any phone calls. I had not told anyone that I was on vacation for a week other than my co-workers and the ladies at the center. So, I would not be disturbed by any unwanted guest. I needed to be by myself. I had just returned from a life lesson journey. And I was exhausted. I knew that I needed my rest to start the work needed around the house, pretty sure that I had slept for about four hours.

Then all of a sudden, I hear loud beating at my door. Almost loud beating like it was the cops or it was big fire in the neighborhood and everyone must come out of their houses.

So I staggered to the door and as I got closer, I heard a woman talking and mumbling curse words and was very angry.

So I tried to peek out of the curtains.

Then she said, "I see you. I know you are there."

So I snatched the door open. I knew that it was Shaquana.

I said, “What do you want?”

She at first thought that I was Roderick because I had just peeked around the door. I was not dressed, so I sorta leaned around. When she thought it was him she said, “Hey,” with a loving voice as if she wanted to see him. But when she realized it was me, she got nasty again. She then told me in a staggering, slurred drunk voice, “He owes me some money.”

I said, “Well, I don't know what to tell you.”

She said, “I’m gonna hold you responsible for it, cause you told me that you would see to it that you would get it for me.”

"Well, that's when we were together. I don't know where he is and you are on your own finding him.”

She said "That's OK, when I start shooting up the house. You’ll see I’m for real.”

And me with a look of sarcasm on my face, just laughed like yeah right.

She said, “OK, God don't like ugly.”

I thought yeah like whatcha doing and I closed my door.

She walked down the steps and I looked out the window and I seen that she had a Thirty-Eight in the back of her pants. I thought what; she does have a gun. I turned and walked towards my bedroom and all of a sudden, I heard three gunshots. I froze in my tracks. But the strange thing is that I didn't duck and run for cover. I felt God was with me. I was not scared, shocked, but scared no. So I then turned and went to look out the window to see if she was still there and she had in fact stopped to talk to my neighbors. I thought to myself this girl has lost her mind. So I tried to get her license plate number, but I couldn't see that far.

I noticed that a neighbor from across the street was out there and I yelled to him to get the plate number. He couldn't hear me, so I started off the porch.

He said, "Mam, she has a gun."

So I stepped back in the house and called the police to make a report. I was sooo pissed off. All the stuff that I had been through; how dare her come and violate my privacy and my home this way. And the fact that I was on vacation for peace and relaxation was really tripping me out.

So after she pulled off, I went across the street to the neighbors, to the house that she was parked in front of, and talked to them.

When the police came, he took their story as to them being a witness to the shootout at high noon. I was able to give them her full name, make and model of the car. And told them she was a resident in Carrollton. She was the one that ran off with my husband to start a new life. I told the police that I hope they find her cause her gun was bigger than theirs. He took all the information and left.

I didn't hear anything else from her after that day.

She had told my neighbors that she was tired of people using her and that she was going to go to jail because she was going to kill somebody. And asked the neighbors to pray for her cause she was ready to go to jail. Well if she comes back around here, she can get that!!!

FEELINGS...

As far back as I can remember I was loved.

Love from my mom, my granny and granddad, my siblings, our neighbors, the little ladies at church, our pastor, my teachers, and my family and friends.

Their warm hugs and kisses. I remember the sense of comfort and the calm of peace.

While I was a child, I can remember the smell in our house, which was the scent from cooking in the kitchen.

I can remember the warm feeling we got as kids. To be the ones in front to take a family photo and how special it made us feel.

Wading in the pool in the back yard…

At the neighborhood park…

Picking pears off the tree in the back yard…

Making taffy in the kitchen…

LIVING IN THE GHETTO!

Every since I chose to live with my grandmother, I've been torn, as far as my living conditions. If I lived with my parents, I would live in an affluent neighborhood with the best of everything. If I lived in the ghetto with my grandparents, I would not have the finer materialistic things and the latest electronic gadget; but I would be surrounded with love and be taught in life how to treat people and turn the other cheek. But in the suburbs, it would be keeping up with the Jones's.

I was torn with shopping at K-Mart with the blue light specials on the West side, or shopping at Lazarus on the East side. That is why I can put on sweats, a t-shirt and sit on the stoop (corner) with the guys, drink beer and talk their language. Then I can go home, put on evening after six attire, and go to the "Brown Hotel, and mix and mingle with the Mayor and his political team, and speak their language. I'm like a chameleon. I can adjust to fit any environment.

Living in the "ghetto" has a lot of history behind it and it's sorta a "roots thang". I have been blessed. I have had the opportunity to live in many parts of the city. And no matter where I live, it's nothing like the ghetto. I feel like its home. I don't have to put on airs and pretend to be something that I'm not. For the most part, I actually feel safe, unlike how the news media tries to portray the West end to be. I 'm quite sure that my grandparents chose the location due to the cost of housing and the fact that there were certain areas where the black families migrated.

The ghetto (the hood) is sooo different from the suburbs. Their way of life is different. Our food is different. Our fast food is different. Our cars and houses are different. We rear our children different. We practice our religion different. We view our lives different.

For an example, when I was growing up, I was taught, and it was across the board with other black families. We were taught, to do all of our laundry on Saturday as well as our chores. No one would leave the house until it was spotless. We were taught that Sunday was for worship, family fellowship and rest. We would in fact, spend our mornings in church, come home to big dinner and then go back to church for evening program. We were taught that there was to be no grass cutting or ironing for that matter on the Lords day (Sunday).

We were also taught to have the utmost respect for our elders and to address them by Mr. & Mrs. We were also taught that if our neighbors had to correct us on our behavior, if they caught us misbehaving, then they had the authority to discipline us. And if our parents found out of our being unruly, then we were destined for more discipline, with no questions asked. It was automatically assumed that the adults were in the right. We were also taught that you were not to wear your welcome out. Meaning, that if you were visiting someone's home you were not to stay too long.

We were also taught, not to curse, and not to use slang words. If we were expressing that someone had lied to us, we were not allowed to actually use the word "lie"- it was considered to be of a foul mouth and considered too "fast" which in fact meant too grown acting and it was inappropriate.

We were also taught that the men in the house were to do all the heavy lifting and moping of the floors. The woman did the housecleaning, the cooking and laundry. We were also taught that a man must honor a woman and he must be considerate of her at all times. We were taught that the man was the head of the house, the provider and the disciplinarian.

We were taught that stealing and lying were the worst that you could do. If you promised to do something, your word was your bond. We were taught that you follow through on any work that you had started until completed.

We were taught that every one was equal, despite what society had set for us. We were taught that being prejudiced was not acceptable and it was not of God. We were taught that honesty was in fact the best policy. We were taught that your character would speak for itself. We were taught that if someone did something against you, to turn the other cheek, as referred to in the Bible.

We were taught that if we didn't believe in God, and have Him as the head of our lives, that life would be considerably harder and more challenging. At a very young age, we believed in God and we worshiped him. We were taught that you must read the Bible to have an understanding and not to allow our Bibles in our homes to just be dust collectors. Black families are very dedicated to their Christian beliefs. We were taught to honor our mothers and fathers because; the Bible says that our days will be longer.

We were taught to have the utmost respect for the cripple and lame. We were taught that if you can't say anything nice, don't say anything at all. We were taught to have respect and look out for our neighbors. We were taught to look out for and protect the other neighbors children by letting them come in your home if they were locked out or give them an after school snack if their parents weren't home yet. We were taught that wives should be submissive to their husbands- within reason (smile).

We were taught not to let them see you sweat on your jobs and not to take too much off of them because you could find work elsewhere. Never go to work if you are ill because you must first take care of you. The job will replace you with someone else, so take care of yourself first. We were taught that if you work hard you can and will have anything that you want in life.

We were taught that if you take one step, in trying to succeed, that God will take two. He just wants to see you trying. We were taught that if you were good and decent here on earth that God has a place prepared for you in heaven upon your death. We were taught that all darkness and bad things were of the devil. We were taught that idle time is the devils workshop, so keep busy at all times trying to better yourself.

We were taught that our children are the future and to train up a child in the way that the Lord would have them to be (Christ-like). We were taught that we are to have respect for the law and people that have been placed in an authority position. We were taught that our homes would represent who we were by cleanliness and everything in decent order.

We were taught that life was what we make it. We were taught that whatever we do, do it to the best of our ability, and do it better than the next person. Master it and own it. We were taught that if you have a conflict with someone, take it to that individual and not gossip about it. Try and deal with it with the person or persons involved. We were taught to love animals. They are God's creations as well. We were taught not to laugh at someone's misfortune, if so, then there you are. We were taught, that if someone wrongs you, that two wrongs don't make it right. And to count your loss and move on, that person will not be successful going around mistreating folks. The vengeance is the Lord's.

SECRETLY SECRETS

Deuteronomy 29:29

Thinking back now that I'm older, I think my mother's drinking had an effect on her moods.

This is not a bashing against my mother, just me trying to merely understand. Also for me to take a look at myself and see if there are any matching traits. Or if it something I can do to better myself and to break the cycle.

Our past generations didn't have all the self-help books or therapist, back in the day like we do now. It is no longer frowned upon if one chooses to seek professional help or self-evaluations. I have spent the majority of the years of my life to try and figure out what went wrong, and how and why. I have also considered that it could be a generational curse placed upon our family as a result of our forefathers or mothers sins. Who knows, I may never know the answers to my questions.

I spoke to my pastor about all of this. He referred me to the scripture in the Bible, Deuteronomy 29:29, that states, the secret things belong to the Lord, and the things He wants reveled to us He will, and he will go a step further and reveal it to our children. So maybe this is a secret thing. This is between God, my mother and me. I hope and pray that the Lord above will reveal it to me.

As the years went on, I was able to get past the hurt and the pain on an obvious level. But ya know, deep inside, it was still there. I just went on as if everything was OK, not realizing the damage that it had caused. The Lord did bless my mom and me to make amends, before her death. She and I had actually become friends. We talked on the phone daily, and laughed and shared and cried. It was weird.

When me and my mom were on good terms, it was on!!! We would talk on the phone for hours, trying to make up for lost time. It was fun. I mean we would talk for three, four, five hours. We both were talkers and we both hogged the conversations and would jockey for position.

I was upset when she passed on because we had just become mother and daughter; and, because it was too soon. She had left me here to take care of my stepfather, the one that she had reservations about. I didn't know how to cope. But, in honor of my mother, I took it upon myself out of the respect of our newfound relationship and the love we had for each other to do as much of the planning of her funeral as I could.

I helped pick out her outfit, took it to the funeral home, viewed her to see if all was in order, insisted that we display her collection of horses, on the alter- because she loved horses, selected that her photo would be in color on the obituary, and anything else I could do.

Now over the years while we were feuding, I didn't visit them much at the house. Besides, it made me feel very uncomfortable, so I missed out on a lot of their parties, and social events. Therefore, I missed the opportunity to meet a lot of their closest friends, neighbors, and acquaintances. So when it came time for us to mingle and socialize at her visitation, and wake, "the viewing", I felt at a lost. I noticed how people were constantly embarrassing my sister Chandra and my dad.

I had lots of friends and associates of my own, co-workers, church members, and my best friend Rosa' Lee. She was truly a blessing at that time. She was right by my side. She knew the pain I was feeling. Rosa' Lee has always been my other sister. I try not to impose on her too often. She has her own family and has things to do but is always ready to lend a helping hand. The Lord has blessed me with a great support system.

But I couldn't help but notice that I was excluded, not because my parents' friends didn't care but because, they really didn't know me. I wanted to SCREAM, "I'M HER DAUGHTER TOO!!!" No one knew I felt as if I would in fact die. I wanted to crawl up and lay next to my mother in the casket and I wanted her to hug me, like she use too when I was a child. I needed her to protect me and be proud of me. To know that even with all the lost time she could still be honored calling me her oldest daughter. It was sooo hard for me, to make it through the night.

So not only was I grieving the death of my mother, my new friend, I was grieving the loss of all those lost years that had gone by. And I would take them back, if the Lord would allow her to just get up. We'd go shopping, dancing, out to dinner, and the movies. We'd go for long walks in the park, hold hands; we would kiss each other, and say that we loved each other every day. We would plan for a bright future together.

The only way of redemption was to give her honor and glory right now, at this moment. To help send her to heaven with a huge celebration, to let her know that all is well. This was not a time for regrets; it was a time for celebration. I wanted to spend this time thanking God for allowing her to be my mother. And even though we had our differences and our problems, she was the only mother I would ever have. She deserved to be honored. This was the lady that would forever be in my daughters' thoughts as their "Granny". I had work to do in making sure that she was represented well and that much respect and honor was in order.

So I had to forget all of my negative thoughts and I went around introducing myself as Susie's oldest daughter. That came with much honor and no one could take that away from me. I needed to show them that I too loved my mother and that I was a nice and kind person as well.

My mom had sooo many people love her. She really did have a great personality and fun loving. She never met a stranger and she kept a house full of guests. My mother had relationships with people that the average person would just ignore. She loved her family and she loved being a mother and a wife. She loved birds and she loved music. She loved fashion and she loved jewelry. She loved to travel and she would try to sing a note or two. She was a spiritual person. Most of all, she loved her grandchildren.

My mother had issues, but who knows, they could have been a product of her upbringing, her past and her childhood. So who are we to judge? I know that my mother is proud of me. She sees my growth and she is honored to call me her oldest daughter!!!

I remember the morning that my mom and I had a conversation about Princess Diana's Death. How we shared that she was so beautiful and special, and how sad the world would be missing her. Well mom...you were sooo special and beautiful and it's sad- how the world is missing you!!!

When my brother and I were growing up, we were inseparable. We did everything together. I was somewhat of a "tomboy". I liked to play basketball and I loved the game of football. I also had a strong liking for track and field. My forte was the fifty and one hundred yard dashes, not too keen with cross-country. I loved being active and having lots of fun.

My brother and I would even coach the kids in our neighborhood. He coached them in football and I coached the little girls in cheerleading. We even competed against other neighborhoods. It was lots of fun. It was sooo cool.

From a young age, I have had the desire to be in charge and be a leader. I have always had ideas, of beginning things and being the first to start this or that. I have always been a creative person, and have always had the desire to be somebody. Ya know, make it big in this ole world, and have my name in lights. Who knows, one day I may even write a book.

My brother and I would hold a banquet at the end of the season for the football players and cheerleaders. We actually awarded them with trophies, gave them acknowledgements and invite their parents for the ceremonies. It was a blast!!!

Our parents always encouraged us to be our best, and to stretch and reach for our dreams. Now my brother was very talented in sports. Everyone that knew him just knew that he would go pro as soon as he would graduate high school. So it was a given, he was being groomed to do so. My brother at a young age played basketball with a lot of the neighborhood greats, like Daryl Griffith, from Louisville Kentucky that went on to play pro ball for the world to see, Bobby Turner and some other Louisville greats. It was so exciting to grow up at such a time when things were so simple and people really had an interest in what the children were doing and didn't mind investing the time and energy in the children. My brother was also brilliant in his studies. He would make straight A's. My brother would score 100pts on a test and he had not even studied. He was just sooo intelligent and wise for such a young age.

At the ripe age of fourteen years old, we knew he was a for sure thing. For whatever he wanted to do in life, if he didn't play sports then he would definitely be a doctor, a lawyer or something with substance.

Myself, I had to study and study on a regular basis to keep my A&B average. As we would continue to grow up, my brother also was the one that would protect me and introduce me to his friends. Then I would meet their sisters. That's how I became popular. I was known as "Robert Johnson's sister". Hardly anyone called me Rhonda. But, my nickname was "RJ". That followed me all my life.

My brother was always hanging out. My brother always won best dressed in school. He dated all the girls that other guys would love to even talk to. He had a winning personality. He was a charmer with his smile. He had it all, good looks, smarts, and athletic ability all rolled into one.

One thing that was really cool about growing up in our old neighborhood was that we lived very close to a drive-in movie theater. We would all go with our families and meet up later that night at the drive in. We would actually have little club meetings at the top of the hill. During intermission, we'd all run back and forth in front of the big screen that seemed to be 1000 feet tall. We would have sooo much fun rolling and doing somersaults down the big hill to go back to our family cars. My neighborhood friends were sooo much fun!!! We did all the quirky things that kids do like hide and seek and red light, green light. We would play pranks on the neighbors like ring doorbells and run and throw water balloons. And just enjoy being kids. It was awesome! Just reflecting back gives such a warm feeling.

I can smell all the cooking. I can taste the warm chocolate chip cookies fresh out of the oven when we'd come home from school to have our after school snack, milk and cookies. Just across the street was a Haywood's Dairy. We'd go over to get ice cream. Just up the road a bit was my girlfriend's parent's neighborhood service station where we'd go and get our candy most of the times free if we would help Mr. Jones do some cleaning around the station. If you go up the road in the other direction and across the street there was Frisch's Big Boy's Hamburger Restaurant. We were in heaven. It was all that we needed.

I can remember the day my brother Robert was to take his longtime girlfriend Pam to her senior prom. He was all dressed up in white tux, with tails, top hat and a cane. He was sharp. We were sooo proud of him. He was on his way and life was his to grab hold to.

He was in a zone. Yeah, he was on his way on his way to jail. He got busted in the bathroom at the prom where he and a few guys snuck off to go and smoke some weed. So, he spent that night in jail. All dressed up and nowhere to go. Boy, he would never live down the jokes from the inmates, the schoolmates and his girl friend. She left him alone a little after that. She saw something coming that we didn't see, the downfall of a future Louisville great.

I MARRIED MY BROTHER

Rodrick and Robert are actually similar in character.

They both do drugs and they both have underlying mental problems. They both are very intelligent. They both are charmers. They both have manipulation down to a science.

They both are stuck in the past. It's always about their past and how they had it going on back in the day. They both will not hold a steady job and think the world owes them.

They both have demonic tendencies. They both have really fowl mouths. They both are punks.

They both can quote you verbatim all the current events in the news. They both think they are sport experts. They don't take God seriously. They don't have a plan for life.

Front and Center

I began working as a clerk for a major healthcare facility about six months before I met Rodrick. I really enjoyed my job and looked forward to making a difference- ya know implementing a new filing system and just adding my flair and style since the predecessor.

Months later, I noticed that my Manager had begun to critique my every move. Now I knew he was a "stickler" upon my accepting the position. Under his direction, I also knew of his military background and the fact that he marched to a different beat- a "micro manage beat". This means he will analyze, miss nothing, and follow by the book. I had high regards for him because he ran a tight ship but a respectable one. So that was fine. I have respect for those in authority.

During my observation, I noticed that he has favorites. And if you don't march to his beat, then there are problems. Opposed to realizing that all workers have a different style. As long as the results are the same and productivity is the same, then what's the problem?

He began to criticize my work and he scrutinized everything. So much so, that I began to get uncomfortable. He has a dry since of humor, and at times, he is actually funny. I think he missed his calling on open mike night at the comedy club. So with my starting to feel uncomfortable, I began to get defensive, as well as paranoid. He always found issues with my work, the data entry part, which I'm solely responsible for. So the spotlight was always on me. He would yell at me in front of other co-workers and summons me to his office by saying, "Front and center." It was very annoying and demeaning to me. I didn't like it. I felt as though he was treating me as a child being summons to the parents' room or principal's office. Basically front and center means, get in my office right now!!!

I have been accused for making errors that have been proven to be computer glitches, and he has never apologized to me. Once I was called on the carpet because I missed too many days in a quarter. It was due to my hysterectomy problems. He literally told me not to miss any more days or I would not have a job, which stressed me and added additional strain on my immune system. To error is human and I have admitted to prior mistakes, some partly carelessness, but most due to lack of concentration.

By being anemic and chronic like myself, it's difficult to concentrate. My blood count was incredibly low. It's a wonder I was able to make it to work, coupled with all the issues going on in my home with Roderick and his drugs, the girls, the dog, and being ill.

Even after it was finally over with Roderick and I, the abuse was no longer in my home but it was on my job. According to the law, it's not considered harassment, if a boss stays on your back or if he just doesn't like you. But to me it's a form of abuse. Bosses aren't just bullies; they're mental abusers. You may as well be living with a rattlesnake. Both will get you.

My boss literally told me that he was going to get me, meaning he'd have the opportunity to fire me. He was going to do his job. I think that employees who are prematurely given power over other employees tend to use their power instead of good management techniques to get people to produce. Some supervisors are no more experienced than the employees they supervise. They don't manage; they just go around being "the boss".

Bullies don't pick fights they can't win; and bully managers always win because they can intimidate with their power to fire you or give raises or bonuses. They manipulate their prey with mind games, which can make their victims feel as helpless as though they were physically threatened. When an employee quits rather than take the continued abuse, the bully figures he's won over a weakling who couldn't do the job right anyway. Abuse or harassment, whatever you want to call it, it is wrong. My boss literally has had me in tears, and has literally made me sick to my stomach. I have had heart palpitations at the notion of hearing his voice.

I have shared my concerns with my dad, granddad and many co-workers. I know that this isn't right. Sometimes a person may not be educated on a particular subject or even have first hand experience, but what you do have is the good old gut feeling. And mine says torment, intimidation, harassment, and just plain old bullshit nit picking because he can, and because she can. They feel as though they can speak to you in any way, any tone, and any manner- and it's wrong.

So with all these feelings, I decided to do something about it. I will no longer give them the power to hurt me or abuse me again. If I lose my job because I take up for myself, oh well. I won't lose my self-respect again.

And don't worry; God wants us to have respect for those in authority. But, they will be held accountable for their actions. And remember, what goes on in the dark comes out in the light, and what goes around comes around. I know!

MY JOURNEY

I learned from this experience that life is too short not to enjoy it. Don't clutter up your life with other peoples baggage. They too have a journey and must travel it alone. It's OK to help others, but God gave me life here on this earth as well. I have my hopes and dreams to pursue and that He will hold me accountable for wasting precious time.

I learned that my children are a gift from God. He's watching how I enjoy my life with them and that He has assigned me to be responsible for them. They are just a loan and that my family is to be honored and respected and appreciated. My friends are special and an extension of his grace.

There is danger of losing control. You must try and stay focused at all times. The forces of darkness are just waiting for you to have a weak moment so the forces can move in. Just like the darkness at the end of a day, it will move in slowly. You may not notice it at first and then all of a sudden- it's here. Keep your guards up and put on the full armor of God to protect you and keep you strong; so that the forces will have no where to come in- and stayed prayed up, meaning to pray. (Ephesians 6:11) Have a close relationship with God so that you will not be vulnerable. I truly believe that if you don't stand for something you will fall for anything and anybody.

Of course, I want to marry the man of my dreams. But now I see that I must first have the same love and ambition towards my God as I do in finding that special someone. I now realize that if I seek first the kingdom of God and his righteousness, then all other things will be added unto me. (Matthew 6:33) There really is a war going on against the forces of good and evil. (Ephesians 6:12) This world has no place for the weak in spirit and the weak minded. So beg the Lord to have favor upon your life. He will enrich you more than you can imagine.

Most people in society have their own issues to deal with. But if you allow yourself to be open and share with others, you can be a tremendous support system to each other. Also not to "should" all over yourself- I should have, could have, all over yourself. When you are in the process of making a decision, take time to decide how you will approach it, or answer it or solve it. Then let it go. If you take out time to process it, then if it should fail or backfire, you then shall have no regrets.

Life is all about choices and the choices that we make. What you're going through (dealing with issues) just know that life is like a puzzle. All the pieces are scattered all over the place. But, piece-by-piece you will be able to pick each issue up and put it in to place. Not long after that, you will be able to hang your puzzle on the wall. I want the Lord to tell me someday, "Well done, my good and faithful servant." (Matthew 25:23)

Ya know this is my journey. And whether people will say one way or another that they would have done this or that, is just comments from the "peanut gallery", because this is my journey. And the choices that I made, good, bad, or indifferent, were mine. I take full responsibility and have no regrets, other than the fact that my children were involved. Then too, it was a life's lesson in the first degree.

And as far as the butterflies, I still love them and they do represent freedom and a free spirit. But the next time I need a sign it will be the Lord guiding me. He doesn't need butterflies to show me which way to go. He just needs me to be obedient!!!

We all have a story to tell. It's just a matter of putting it in writing form for publication. I say if you have a yearning, like I did, to tell your life story- then... start writing and write now!!!

For the ladies that want to pass judgment and wonder why I would allow such horror into the life of my children- don't pass judgment. Because if you do then there you are, all of a sudden you will fall prey to something that will have you totally hypnotized. So just realize that this is my journey and not yours. Never say never. And be careful to whom you gossip about, because you could be next!!!

LIFE...

Life is a gift from the Lord above,
and he gives it in hopes that we make
a difference in someone else's life.
It is for us to enjoy by helping others and to be in it,
Be a part of it,
To feel it,
To share it,
And to know it,
Own it.
Make your life your job and do the best you can:
Learn
Breath
Smell
Touch
Experience
Hold
Reach
Hug
Love it
Life will last but awhile.
Let it know that you're here and that you're near.

HONOR

When I think of honor, I think of myself. I would like to honor myself at this moment. I have had an interesting life so far, and I think that I have handled all of this with honor. I think that you must play the game of life with the cards that are dealt to you. I think that I have been able to maintain a sound mind and have not fallen to the negativity that I could have held onto.

I honor myself for doing the best that I could with what I had. I will continue to celebrate life and continue to be a lady no matter what comes my way. I know that I will be able to work through it because I have the grace of God, upon me. I honor myself for getting out of a marriage that was not healthy- it was belittling. I honor myself, for keeping a great attitude and standing steadfast in what I believe.

I honor myself for staying with what I was taught as a child and being patient with the obstacles that were set before me. I honor myself for loving my children enough to keep going on, not giving up, and not giving in. I honor myself for not being so self-absorbed, having constant consideration for others and being happy for my friends, their accomplishments and being a support system to them. I honor myself for encouraging my daughters to have relationships and allowing themselves to trust.

I'm honoring myself for allowing myself to be free to love again and not be stifled by the negativity that has been a part of my life so far with men. I honor myself for always trying again and again, for not quitting at the first sign of opposition. I honor myself for being a great friend because I know that in order to have great friends; one must first be a great friend.

I honor myself for not holding grudges and for letting go- opposed to holding on to anger and letting it control me or reduce me to a level that is not acceptable in God's eye. I honor myself, for having the courage, for seeking help and knowing that something must be done. I honor myself for being brave enough to face my fears and take on new challenges.

I honor myself for not being a materialistic person and having an appreciation for the simple things in life. I honor myself for being able to be open and truly have no secrets. I honor myself for being a good listener. I honor myself for being a hard worker. I honor myself for enjoying life and trying to reach new heights. I honor myself for learning how to hear and accept ideas and suggestions from others whom I know mean me well.

I honor myself for not allowing current circumstances to sour my religious convictions, to still believe in God and to know that he has my back at all times. I honor myself for learning to respect others privacy and not taking it personal if they are not as open with their life and circumstance as I am to others. I honor myself for being an inspiration to others and for allowing them to be themselves in my presence.

I honor myself for always looking for ways to make others happy- within reason. I honor myself for being a nice person and not having to apologize for actually being happy. I honor myself with music. I love to treat myself to a new CD every now and then. I honor my weight at it's current level and realize that it too has a place and a time.

I honor myself for being the best mother that I know how to be. I honor myself for being the best daughter that I know how to be. I honor myself for having integrity and self-respect. I honor myself for working on my self-esteem and self-love.

I honor myself for having a love for children. I honor myself for having respect for my elders. I honor myself for having regards to authority. I honor myself for being an excellent neighbor.

And, I honor myself for being me!

Stepfather

Thank you for stepping up to the plate,
not really knowing what all it would take.
You were young and in love,
full of hope from heaven above.
Not too sure where to start,
but it would definitely come from the heart.
You first embraced us with a tight strong hug,
that's when I knew it was true love.
A young man then a father of two,
just over night from speaking the words…I Do.
Many were in doubt that you would take such a route too young of a man,
to take such a chance, but you took a stand.
You stepped out faith was the key,
praying daily on your knees.
Years would go by; you'd help us grow
playing ball and teaching us to throw.
Birthdays, proms, graduations
were all filled with your love and salutations.
We've laughed and cried
but you stood by our sides,
an open heart and a checkbook too.
Without you what would we do?
Just as you have watched us grow
we have watched you explode!!!
Explode into a man so great
with a heart as big as our state.

You have survived the death of your first wife with lots of tears and lonely nights.

Now you are ready to reach new heights,

You deserve the best for the rest of your life.

A stepfather, WOW!!!

Daddy, please take your bow!!!

Happy Father's Day

FLASHBACKS

Ouch, that hurt! All of a sudden, I had that feeling of hurt and anger again. It will rear its ugly head from time to time. The hurt I felt when I first realized the mind games and manipulation that my husband, not only used on me and my kids, but how he did Rashida and her children.

She and I use to talk on the phone in between the breakups of Roderick and myself, as well as their breakups. Don't think for a minute that it was the two minds of us women trying to bust him. It was just the times that we were both trapped by his antics and really were out to find out things from each other and share our experiences with each other. She told me stories of how he would not like for her to spend time or money, for that matter, on her kids. And he used the same phrases on her like me. He would say such things as "Your kids are spoiled," and, they don't deserve this or that. He would use whatever the children would confide in him, the rare occasions of that, and use it against them. He would also act liked a spoiled child if he didn't get his way.

We would exchange comments that he made to me and Rashida. They were almost word for word. For an example with him going back and forth between the two of us, he would get our names mixed up. Ya know call me Rashida and her Rhonda. That was my way of always knowing if they had been talking. If they were messing around, he'd do it repeatedly. If they had just been sneaking on the phone, he'd mess up here and there, but not as often.

To show you how naive I still was I thought that considering the fact that she and I shared such pain, and on the same level, that we could actually bond. But, she specifically told me that she could never be my friend and that the only thing we had in common was him. Now this woman was the one that we would talk on the phone for hours. Ya see, he played us against each other so... that if he stayed out all night I would assume he was with her and vice versa. So there were times that we both would break down and call the other.

I can remember her and I conversing over long conversations, for an entire week. Of course, she'd never admit to such. And there were times that I would call her and tell her that he had been over my house and he was on his way to her house. We'd talk in between his travels. She was sooo street smart unlike myself, that what we had talked about before his arriving to her house went all away the moment he walked in the door. She would say, "Someone wants to talk to you," and give him the phone. I could have just died. I couldn't believe that she set me up like that. But after that, I learned how to play the games too. In some cases, I'm a quick study.

I have always loved to read, and nowadays, you can pull up anything and print it off the Internet. I would pull up and print out sections on marriage, relationships, and signs of a bad marriage and brainwashing. Well I honestly think that my husband would read the articles and use them against me. He would watch all those shows on TV about the same topics and he had all day to sit and think of ways to manipulate me and my daughters. He told me one day to stop reading all those articles. I was stupid for reading it and I needed to be in the "real world" and to stay out of the fantasy life. I told you he was smart.

Oh, and not to mention nosey. One of the symptoms of being bi-polar and schizophrenic was paranoia. Always thinking someone was against him and set out to hurt or have one up on him. Just flashing back again, he always hated when I would go off into my daughter's rooms and we'd have mother-daughter talks. When I would come out he'd say," You always got secrets and so now everything is private." I would just look at him as if he was crazy, and rightfully so.

HEARSAY...

The interesting thing that I have had to succumb to is the backlashing of my ex-husband. I keep hearing things from people that are just unreal. He likes to play the martyr. He loves to go around telling people that I hit him and that he's not a violent person.

Well the records down at the courthouse say different, and that was twenty years ago. We had not met. The mere fact that it is on record that his first wife received her divorce on the grounds of domestic violence, adultery, mental cruelty, and niggerness is enough said.

The associates and friends that know me realize that I had been provoked to such behavior. If anyone had been subjected to as much as I did in the three years that we were together would definitely understand. Opposed to him just saying, we just couldn't make it work, is too easy. He has to tell the story so that I look like the bad girl.

But, my reputation and my character speak for itself. So no matter what he puts out in the street, the street also know of his past. And, the streets know that I tried over and over again to make our marriage work. So the hell with him and his little sad pathetic version of what happened to the fall of our ten-month marriage made in hell.

It has also been implied that I did crack as well. Ya know birds of feathers flock together. Well no sense in trying to convince anyone. I know and God knows that I have never used the stuff- only just amazed how powerful it is, and that it will ruin your life. It's not a good feeling for people to think that of me. But, I have been accused of worse.

Part of the domestic violence is manipulation and mind altering. The fact that he would provoke me until I hit him was a part of the plan. Then he'd have cause to protect his self. We are talking about a master of manipulation and a mind altering professional. My ex-husband had this down to science. He knew what to do and how to do it. He knew how far he could go what, would stand up in court and what would send him to jail. He was very intelligent. He knew the ins and outs of the law. The one thing he didn't know is that one day, I would wake up and it would be over!!!

Actually, this whining makes him look like a punk going around crying and looking for attention. It's funny that none of his partners believes him. We just laugh about him being out of the picture.

NO SIGNS

I don't want any signs of his existence. I decided to redecorate the house. I don't want anything in the house that represents that he was even here. I want all the walls painted, even if it's not needed. I want our home to represent purity in the best way. I want everything white or colorful, nothing that would exude negativity.

Any furniture that he had or anything that would even come close to the dreadful memories, new curtains and carpet, new art work, new silk flowers, new dishes, new everything. Little by little, I will erase the bad memories that this beautiful home once had. I will open all the windows and blinds and show that life exists around here.

All the demonic spirits that was once lurking will be gone. I will go in every room, pray, and ask the Lord to dwell here and that He will place a hedge of protection around this home to protect me and my girls. I'm saving the repair of the busted hole in the wall placed by his fist, as the grand finale. It will mark the new life that now is present within theses walls: peace serenity, and joy. Then I will be able to close the chapter in the book of being "whooped".

Last night I started to paint over the bathroom walls that he painted. I tried very hard to cover all the pink that was on the walls last year. I went into every crack and every crevice I could reach. I want to make sure that there is no trace of him left behind.

Now I don't wish anything bad on him. I'm not like that. However, I want nothing to remind me of my past three years of hell. And if a gallon of white paint can wash away, some of the stinge that was left behind, then I will paint until there are no more signs. I wish that I could close my eyes and he would be nonexistent in my mind. Sorta a bad nightmare, and then reality sets in and I wake up and realize it was just a nightmare and none of those things really happened.

THE AFTERMATH

After assessing the damage, it was like an earthquake had hit my life. As I looked around to see all the destruction, the hurt and pain felt by me and the girls, it was immeasurable. It was an eight on the Rictor scale. I sat back and looked over the photos of memories of the good times, family get-togethers and such.

My heart was shattered and cracked. But, the foundation was still there. I had God. Everything was like scattered debris. We had to clean it up: broken feelings, broken spirits, confusion, despair, unbelief, a catastrophe, feelings of being lost, the nasty feeling of being violated and a sense of white pure snow disturbed by unwanted footprints. This definitely was cause to be deemed a national disaster by the Federal Government. Emergency funds and the Red Cross needed to be included to get this place back together. Things could be fixed, cosmetically speaking, but the structure was truly damaged. The fact that the foundation was still standing gave some hope of re-building. But the thoughts, the memories, and the pain will take a while.

It's amazing how such a force of wind coming from the wrong directions and at the wrong time, can almost destroy such a beautiful place created by God. With God's grace and wisdom, I will be able to handle any storm, tornado, or hurricane that may come my way. So I will continue to trust and have faith in GOD!!!

As I began to pick up every emotion, piece-by-piece, I began to redesign things. I wanted to start with some fresh and new, and others could be taped and glued. For example being more observant was the first thing I needed to attack. Because not being aware of red flags is the key to open many doors that should never be opened in the first place. Another was not being sooo vulnerable because it can set you up for failure. Another is to not be sooo trusting. Another is to stay focused and not be side tracked. Another is to be true to myself. Another is to not ever put anything or anyone before God. Another is to honor myself as being worthy of the right kind of love and that I count too!

REVENGE

When I think of the word "revenge," I think of power and paybacks. I think of ways I can prevail in paying someone back for whatever I deem as being wrongly done to me. I think of seeing that person getting their just desserts. In Buddhist teaching, the law of Karma says," For every event that occurs, there will follow another event whose existence was caused by the first. Meaning, what goes around, comes around. It will. I may not be around to witness it per say, but it will happen. Just the mere thought of thinking it would ensure its outcome. So I must rely on good ole wise sayings and go on with my life.

To me, the real revenge is survival and living to tell my story. The fact, that I did not die at the hands of the abuser and the obvious fact that he had not destroyed my spirit to go on. So, the best revenge is none.

Just continue to be who you are and your life will change. Just seconds after you decide to start a new life and take back control of your well-being and your destiny- just as sure as you're sitting here reading- great things are happing in your life right now. Remember that you're special. You're one of a kind. We have something to offer back to the world as a participant in this world. It's your job to find out what your participation will be. How will you make a difference in someone's life? What legacy will you leave for your family, friends, children, and generations to come? We all have a gift. Find yours. Fine tune it and share it.

Start the job that you have always wanted.

Start painting- and this time try to sell it to your friends and family. Art speaks and people listen to what it has to say or they will at least interrupt it to say what they may think it says.

Start that diet that you promised yourself years ago that you would.

Take up karate for exercise.

Take a self-defense course to learn how to protect yourself if someone gets in your space.

Or, start practicing with the family recipes and make a cookbook.

Just get busy starting your new life!!! Now!!!

NAME CALLING

I remember once after a big fight and break up; Roderick had come to the house to get his clothes after my putting him out. When he came to the door, he called me a" barrel built B" referring to my body shape. To my amazement, the body shape was only an issue if I was ending our relationship. All the other times he said nothing, only if he was not having his way.

So when people and children say sticks and stones don't hurt, they do. The abuser is an expert at minimizing the verbal abuse. Domestic Violence is about control, as I have said many times. When the abuser feels that he is losing his control, he literally loses control. Domestic violence is about the control of one human being to another. This control begins with verbal abuse and is similar to mind control.

Mind control is the shaping of a person's attitudes, beliefs, and personality without a person's knowledge or consent. Mind control employs deceptive and surreptitious manipulation. Mind control works by gradually exerting increasing control over individuals through a variety of techniques, such as repetition of routine activities, intense humiliation or sleep deprivation.

Verbal abuse attacks one's spirit and sense of self. Verbal abuse attempts to create self-doubt. "You don't know what you're talking about." "You don't have a sense of humor." "You can't take a joke" "You're too sensitive." "You're crazy."

Verbal abuse also controls one's mind. Some women who have left a verbally and sometimes physically abusive relationship twenty or more years of age still find themselves wondering, "Maybe there's something I could have done..." or "Maybe if I'd tried to explain just one more time my relationship/marriage would have gotten better." Very often, the people who find themselves the target of controlling behaviors can't comprehend that anyone would want to control them, so they try to be nice. This doesn't work. You can't stop a rapist by being extra nice.

VIOLENCE BEGETS VIOLENCE

Because the victim is so unheard, so belittled, so undermined, there comes a time when they too might lash out in violence (physical or verbal). Usually this is after trying to communicate in every other fashion, being coerced or pushed so hard for so long- literally being ridden like a horse by the abuser- that the victim will retaliate. ***With that, the abuser is happy you have now achieved just what the abuser wanted and has been looking for. They can now say to the victim, "Yes, but you have been violent too."***

This is a very dangerous trap for those who try to take responsibility for their own lives. One thinks "Well, I have...I am no better than he. I have struck out. I too have hurt and therefore, I must be more understanding of his rages." This is very dangerous and very subtle! But the pain, constant undermining and belittling/mimicking took their toll. I could no longer hold back. I did hit him many times. But this was of not my character and I'm not a violent person. Sometimes it felt good to hit him; but he would just beat it out of me later or take it out on my daughters. So it's not good- ***violence begets violence.***

More and more organizations that help the victims of battering realize that verbal abuse precedes domestic violence. ***Thousands of battered people have said that the hurt of verbal abuse lasted longer than the bruises of physical abuse.*** Verbal abuse is a kind of violence that creates a deep emotional pain and mental anguish that can be immobilizing. If you are in a verbally abusive relationship and need a support group, whether or not you have been battered, I recommend that you call your local Domestic Violence Center, to find out where a group meets near you to meet your needs.

I was having a conversation with a friend of mine just the other day and she stated that her fiancé had never called her names. He only got mad and yelled at her on occasions. ya know if he was tired or if he had a bad day. My heart just sunk. She has no clue. All I ask is that you be true to yourselves, and ***just think how these comments sound from other victims that are in denial***.

He told me that he would kill me if I didn't straighten up. But, he sent me flowers the next day.

He never hits me. When he curses me, I can tell he's sorry. It's just a habit. They curse a lot on his job.

We always go to the movies and out to dinner. He always picks the movies and the restaurants.

It's OK; at least we get to go somewhere!

He blocked me so I couldn't leave the house. But later we made love and made up.

I know he does illegal things, but he makes a lot of money and we live very good. We want for nothing. So, I don't ask questions about all those checks coming in the mail or those boxes in the garage. Besides, it's his business and he would get angry if I was to ask.

He threw me down on the bed and held me until I said, "Yes I would have sex." We had a nice night after all.

I know he hates my children, but that's because he's not use to little children and all that noise.

He smacked me once but it was not really that hard. And he swore on the Bible he'd never do it again.

He pushed me down, and I fell at a party and he yelled at me and told me to get my fat ass up. But, the drive home was OK. We talked things out.

Even though he tried to kill me, I know it's just the drugs. If he gets help, we will save our marriage.

He said that my children were spoiled and lazy, but he does nothing to help out around the house. But he will soon, when I get my kids straight.

He just smokes crack on the weekends, but he's not really into drugs.

He makes comments of my weight and how I may look this summer in my bathing suit. But he eats us out of house and home.

He says stuff like don't eat that, your thighs are too big now. But I know he loves me. I gave him two beautiful children.

He buys me anything I want from diamonds to furs. All he wants is for me to look nice and not speak too much when we have company.

He beats me but he learned that from watching his dad.

He flirts with other women, but he's going home with me.

Even though he yells and calls me names, I know he loves me. We've been together for ten years. When he calls me names, I just laugh because I know I'm not. It doesn't bother me!

My husband is always late picking me up from work. He just gets caught up with his buddies.

He always apologizes.

My friend says that men cheat all time and for me to just find a man to cheat with and we will be even. Just as long as he takes care of home, meaning me and the children and our well-being. It's just the way life is. All the good men are taken.

He thinks a woman should be seen and not heard. So I just let him do most of the talking. I'm a good listener!

He wants sex everyday, sometimes three or four times a day. He wants me to always be ready. I know he's not cheating on me.

Where would he find the time? He wants me to try new things, but I'm not interested. But I will so we can stay happily married.

He comes from a family of abuse, but he won't lay a hand on me. He loves me too much!

We have all being in denial at one time or another. But just stop and listen to some of the things that we say to ourselves and others and think how it really sounds. Pay attention to what is really going on and what is really being said…

Will you allow your mate to call you a"B" or "W"? Which one? Which is best? Which describes you most? Name calling starts out little and ends up being destructive!!!

ABUSE IS ABUSE

Domestic Violence can take different forms, but its goal is always the same. Batterers want to control their domestic partners through fear. They do this by regularly abusing them verbally, mentally, physically, emotionally, financially and sexually. Here are some of the forms domestic violence can take.

VERBAL, MENTAL, PHYSICAL, EMOTIONAL, FINANCIAL, SEXUAL- all are violations of a person.

Verbal Abuse- Constant criticism, making humiliating remarks, not responding to what the victim is saying, mocking, name-calling, yelling, swearing, interrupting or changing the subject

Physical Abuse- Hitting, slapping, kicking, choking, pushing, punching or beating

Emotional Abuse- Not expressing feelings, not giving compliments, not paying attention, not respecting the victim's feelings, rights, and opinions or not taking the victim's concerns seriously

Financial Abuse- "Economic Control" Not paying bills, refusing to give the victim money, not letting the victim work, interfering with the victim's job or refusing to work and support the family

Sexual Abuse- Forcing sex on an unwilling partner, demanding sexual acts that the victim does not want to perform or degrading treatment

Isolation- Making it hard for the victim to see friends and relatives, reading the victims mail, controlling where the victims goes, taking the victims car keys

Coercion- Making the victim feel guilty, pushing the victim into decisions, sulking, manipulating children and other family members, always insisting on being right, making up impossible "rules" and punishing the victim for breaking them

Harassment- Following or stalking, embarrassing the victim in public, constantly checking up on the victim or refusing to leave when asked

Abusing Trust- Lying, breaking promises, withholding important information, being unfaithful, being overly jealous or not sharing domestic responsibilities

Threats or Intimidation- Threatening to harm the victim, the children, family members and pets, using physical size to intimidate; shouting or keeping weapons and threatening to use them

Self-destructive Behavior- abusing drugs, alcohol, threatening self-harm, or suicide, driving recklessly, deliberately doing things that will cause trouble (like telling off the boss)

SELF-ESTEEM

I can remember several people over the years express to me that I had low self-esteem. For the life of me, I just couldn't understand. So, I just assumed that they didn't know what they were talking about or they were just confused. Because I love myself and I'm happy with who I have become. Sooo, what's the deal? Well, I have decided to take on the challenge and break down the words, self-esteem, to myself, for myself, to see myself.

To understand self-esteem, it helps to break the term into two words. Let's take a look at the word esteem First, esteem (say: ess-**teem**) is a fancy word for thinking that someone or something is important or valuing that person or thing. For example, if you really admire your friend's dad because he is a volunteer at the fire department, it means that you hold him in high esteem. And the special trophy for the most valuable player on a team is often called an esteemed trophy. This means the trophy stands for an important accomplishment.

And self means- well, yourself! So when you put the two words together, it's easier to see what self-esteem is. It's how much you value yourself and how important you think you are. It's how you see yourself and how you feel about your achievements. Self-esteem isn't bragging about how great you are. It's more like quietly knowing that you're worth a lot (priceless, in fact!). It's not about thinking you're perfect- because nobody is- but knowing that you're worthy of being loved and respected.

Good self-esteem is important because it helps you to hold your head high, feel proud of yourself, and what you can do. It gives you the courage to try new things and the power to believe in yourself. It lets you respect yourself, even when you make mistakes. When you respect yourself, others respect you, too.

Having good self-esteem is also the ticket to making good choices about your mind and body. If you think you're important, you'll be less likely to follow the crowd if your friends are doing something dumb or dangerous. If you have good self-esteem, you know that you're smart enough to make your own decisions. You value your safety, your feelings and your health- your whole self! Good self-esteem helps you know that every part of you is worth caring for and protecting.

There are choices and circumstances that affect our self-esteem level as well. One-night stands, dating a married man, being raped, falsely accused, domestic violence, drugs, alcohol, toxic people in your life and no spiritual connection.

You can't touch it, but it affects how you feel. You can't see it, but it's there when you look at yourself in the mirror. You can't hear it, but its there every time you talk about yourself. What is this important, but mysterious thing? It's your self-esteem!

So it was not that I was in denial, or maybe I was (smile). But, it also had to do with just not understanding the definition of self-esteem. So if you're being told this or that by some trusted friends, it wouldn't hurt to check into it and see what you can find out about yourself. Real friends care and real friends want the best for their friends.

Thanks Mrs. Ruby, and thank you Shellie (smile).

What It Means To Unlearn

When I sit back and go over all that has happened or that I have been exposed to, I realize that a lot of my thinking has to change. But, how do I change all those nights and days of the verbal abuse? How do I get it out of my head?

First, I must want to change my thought process. I must want to remove all negatives and replace them with positives.

Some would assume that I know better not to adopt the name-calling. It shouldn't be taken personal. Being called out of my name on a regular basis has in fact played over and over in my mind like a record.

So, first I choose to remove people and negative things in my life.

I choose to listen to inspirational and instrumental music and free my mind.

Then, daily I would remind myself how special I am and that God loves me.

The brain stores things. Limited in what it can hold, the brain needs to be emptied before I can add more knowledge. I must "empty the vessel".

Over time, new thoughts will surface and become regular thoughts.

I must be able to step outside of my old thoughts and realize that there are other ways of seeing and believing.

I must awaken myself and be free to choose.

REVELATION

People don't understand, why I'm such a happy person considering all the things I have been through. But, it's only by God's grace and his mercy. I'm a living testimony that people do love you. Families do the best with what they have. And that life is a pleasure and a privilege. So enjoy!!! Keep your head up and I'll see you on the other side of glory.

TO MY DAUGHTERS

I first want to apologize for the hurt and pain that I caused you, for my mistakes and the bad choices that I made in my life. I take full responsibility for my actions and I ask that you forgive me. Know that being a parent does not come with a manual or a handbook, but it does come with the Christian upbringing that was instilled in me at an early age. I have tried to pass that on to the both of you. My legacy to you is love, Christian beliefs and the concept of following your gut feeling that the Lord has equipped us with. Always follow your deep down inside feelings. It is God's way of showing you which way to go. I hope and pray that I will live long enough to see and get to know my grandchildren. But if not, know that I love you and that I will always be with you!!!

Gigi

I'm sorry for the pain. I'm sorry that I didn't hold you. I'm sorry that I was not there for you. God puts people in the right place at the right time, and you had an angel there with you, Mrs. Elaine. She was my eyes. When she held you, it was me holding you too. I'm sorry that I put you in the environment that has caused you such agony, but you are strong just like me. Together we will draw strength from each other. I love you and you have brought me such joy. I only hope that you know it was not my fault and that I would do nothing to hurt you. When he threw you against the wall, I didn't even realize what had happened. It was all so fast. I was too busy trying to protect Chanielle, my daughter. I didn't even see what had happened to you until it was too late. Forgive me, Mommie. I love you Gigi, the best dog in the world. I know you were trying to protect us and you got hurt in the process. I'm sorry. I love you!!!

WALKING HOME

I had just got off the number, twenty-five bus on the way home from work. I always take a short cut through the alley- it's in the back of my house. Most people would not because it is truly a sight to see. People used the back alleys for dumping their old trash and old tires that they cannot use any longer. I was not scared, just disgusted.

So, as I was strolling, I was thinking to myself, how a dear friend of mine, named Glenn had met the woman of his dreams. He had told of a story of how she was just walking down the street that he lived on, they just struck up a conversation, and it went on from there. They have been married for about eight years now and they have two beautiful daughters. A big smile came across my face and thought to myself, that it was sooo sweet. If things were only just that simple these days!

Just as I began to look up, I saw a guy coming my way and he had a big grin on his face as if we had meet somewhere before. He stated that I should not be walking in the alley this late into the evening. I laughed because it was still daylight so I knew that it was a line. He was calling himself trying to get to know me better. I was really tired, but he was cute. So, I gave him some conversation and the next thing you know we had been talking for thirty minutes. Then we walked around to my house and sat down on the front porch. We then talked and talked and talked and mentioned the places that we had seen each other- in the neighborhood.

But it was just amazing to us how we met. I was thinking to myself that it was tooo weird that I'd meet him just after thinking about how Glenn had met his wife. Then I met Darryl, of course not thinking anything of it. But it was a chance meeting and the odds were great. The fact that he and I go that way all the time, but had never seen each other, just trips me out to no end.

We ended up talking and laughing as if we had known each other for years. It was obvious that we had an interest with other, but all I could hear in the back of my head was that it was too soon and not to even go there. So I just watched him while he was talking. I paid close attention to the way he would pronounce each word, in hopes that I would find something wrong with him, because my heart was too fragile. No way was I going to put myself through any more pain.

While he was talking, I was so infatuated with his looks. Now to me, he's cute. I felt the same attraction to my husband for some reason. So I had to check myself because Roderick was not cute. Most of the people couldn't see what I saw in him. But, I saw a person. This time with Darryl, I see handsome, mature and tall. He looked sooo good to me that I couldn't focus.

I had to push myself because I would always fall for a guy that just gave me attention. This time was going to different. I wanted him to know me and what I was about and not sooo much him. This was about me. I have a right to be selective and not take the first guy that came my way or would show some sign of interest. He had to get into me, learn me and know me. It was not for me to get to know him first. I could learn all that by listening too-, which I had not done before. I would always jump the gun and take off running. Next thing ya know I was in love with someone that didn't know what was important to me or didn't even care how I felt on issues. So this time is to be different.

Darryl is about 6'3", medium build, has a nice grade of hair, and it's mixed black and gray. I would love to see him in a tux. He'd look like a million dollar man. His presence is so grand. His walk is extraordinary and he's bow-legged. Ahhhh, he's sexy to me! And that's all that counts.

Now I just have to figure out how to be in a relationship again with out losing my focus and my dreams. That night Darryl said that he would call. I have to be truthful; I wanted him too. But with all the disappointments of late, if he didn't call I wouldn't be surprised. I was tired of trying to read into things and make up thoughts in my head and daydream of men. I just had to wait and see what would happen. After our long conversation, if he's interested he will call. For the first time in my life I didn't sit by the phone, I went on with my life. I wasn't checking to see if the phone was working, if the sound was turned up or picking up the phone for a dial tone. I just went on about my business.

Before you knew it, the phone rang and it was Darryl. Of course, I was happy, but I had mixed emotions. I immediately went into the mode of, "What's his story and what's his hang up?" All those old feelings of being used and abused came back. So again, I had to check myself and stay focused. I wasn't so scared of a new relationship, but I knew that I'd have to be careful. The most precious things close to my heart were my daughters. It would take a hell of a man to even be allowed in my home or even have the honor or privilege to meet my daughters. For they too, had experienced at a young age, the hurt and pain of bad marriage, of abuse and torment. So I had precious cargo and this train wasn't moving no way soon without protection, assurance, and guidance.

Darryl and I had the typical first few conversations on the phone like other couples. Ya know, what's your sign? (hahaha) What is your favorite food? Where do you like to go? What church do you attend? Who's your favorite singing group? I noticed that we held one another's attention. We made each other laugh, so it was a start. But come on now, I need more.

I was not into guiding a guy the way you'd like for him to go. This time would have to be different. He'd have to come with something to the table. No more of my setting up the table and having everything readily available. No more of my being the relationship instructor. I was just gonna sit back and see what he had planned. If he could in fact, appreciate friendship and the maturity of just getting to know me and not wanting to jump in the bed. I was hoping that he would not mess up. He seems like a good catch, but I was not giving any clues as to how he should do this or that. If it was meant to be, he had to do everything right and in time; he will meet the approval of my heart and soul.

Upon our talking on the phone, Darryl asked if I would mind if he'd cut my grass because it needs to be cut once again before the winter sets in. Well hell, good question!!! He scored a few points there because I have tried to get someone to cut that backyard, for months. I couldn't even pay anyone. No one wanted to tackle the long, backyard and all that hard work. But, Darryl stated that he wanted too. And, that he had all the equipment. Equipment, wow! The other guys said I needed a riding mower and I needed this or that. Darryl said that he has it all. I was starting to think, yeah, you do (smile).

Self-check. Slow down, Rhonda! Don't fall for this. Yes you need the yard done, but don't get all excited over this. He has to do more than this. So slow your row and calm down.

So I agreed and told him that I would really appreciate it if he'd do the yard. So he said that he would do it the next day. So we hung up and I was happy. I was sitting at my desk and I had begun to think of how to approach this newfound friendship. How I could, in a nice way, express how I felt and to get everything upfront and to stay focused. So, being the creative person that I am, I decided to write him a poem.

I know to some, it may seem silly. But to me, poetry is important. And, it is important for the man in my life to have a keen sense of the art of writing, to think much broader and to have an interest in some of the things that I love like music- especially jazz, reading, writing and plays and productions. Those are things in my life that make me feel good. If too many days go by and I don't allow myself the time to read, I get uncomfortable. I have a longing for it and must take out that special time for myself to relax and learn more. So I sat down to write a poem that would express my feelings up till this point. This is what I wrote.

You & Me

What a difference a day makes.
A positive attitude is all it takes.
Your smile, your laugh and your grin
Definitely shines from within.

You say that it's meant to be.
I say let it happen naturally.
If it's from heaven above,
Then you and me will fall in love.
Let's take it slow and let our friendship grow,
And then you and me will know.

Tonya Jordan

Darryl really seems like a nice man. I'm sure he will make some woman very happy. But, after a few months of being on a journey, I knew I was not ready for a serious relationship. I must stay focused and begin the long awaited bond with God that I had put off for so many years. I want to now spend time with God and help do his work.

I will no longer look at life through rose-colored glasses. I love the color rose, but it is tinted and somewhat shaded. I will look at life with clarity, because with clarity comes power. And besides, I must be very careful because…Just beyond my heart lies my soul.

Resource Page

Factnet

www.factnet.org 9/26/2003

Buddhism

www.ncf.carleton 11/3/2003

Bible

King James Version

Domestic Violence National Association

Poem

Anais Nin

* Special thanks to the Louisville Free Public Library (Shawnee branch)

Look For:

Tonya Jordan's
Next Novel

Adventures of Buttercup & Butterbug

A Children's Book on Domestic Violence